JIMMY'S
STARS

ALSO BY MARY ANN RODMAN

Yankee Girl

JIMMY'S STARS

MARY ANN RODMAN

FARRAR, STRAUS AND GIROUX

NEW YORK

www.fsgkidsbooks.com

Library of Congress Cataloging-in-Publication Data
Rodman, Mary Ann.
    Jimmy's stars / Mary Ann Rodman.— 1st ed.
        p.   cm.
    Summary: In 1943, eleven-year-old Ellie is her brother Jimmy's "best girl," and
when he leaves Pittsburgh just before Thanksgiving to fight in World War II, he
promises he will return, asks her to leave the Christmas tree up until he does, and
reminds her to "let the joy out."
    ISBN-13: 978-0-374-33703-2
    ISBN-10: 0-374-33703-9
    1. World War, 1939–1945—Juvenile fiction.   [1. World War, 1939–1945—Fiction.
2. Brothers and sisters—Fiction.   3. Soldiers—Fiction.   4. Family life—
Pennsylvania—Fiction.   5. Schools—Fiction.   6. Pittsburgh (Pa.)—History—
20th century—Fiction.]   I. Title.

PZ7.R6166 Jim 2008
[Fic]—dc22

                                                                    2007005091

For my beloved aunt and uncle, Agnes Smith Neofes
and Jim Smith, and my mother, Frances Smith Rodman

JIMMY'S STARS

1

The two people Ellie McKelvey hated most were Adolf Hitler and Victoria Gandeck. Hitler lived in Germany, but Victoria was just across the alley. And right now, Ellie hated Victoria more.

After all, it was Victoria's fault.

Ellie had been minding her own beeswax, thinking about the arithmetic homework she needed to do before the end of lunch hour. Then, as she crossed the schoolyard, sucking peanut butter from her teeth, Victoria yelled that horrible word. "Slacker! Ellie's brother is a yellow-bellied slacker!"

The next thing Ellie knew, she was sitting outside the principal's office with bruised knuckles and the metallic taste of blood in her mouth. Victoria was sprawled in the chair beside her, a bloody hanky to her nose, outstretched legs taking up half the room.

She's going to have a shiner, Ellie thought with satisfaction. But then I probably will too. She rubbed her sore scalp. Victoria had jerked her to the ground by her braids. She wondered if this was what getting scalped felt like.

Dust swirled in the sunbeams streaming through the office windows. It was a blue-sky-good-things-will-happen kind of day, more summer than September. TODAY IS FRIDAY, SEPTEMBER 10, 1943, said the Pittsburgh School Supplies calendar next to the window. Too nice a day to be in trouble.

B-r-r-i-n-n-n-g. The bell ending lunch hour.

Trampety tramp tramp tramp. Four hundred pairs of feet marched in line, down the hall, past the open door of the office. When the line paused for a minute, two little girls giggled, pointing at Ellie and Victoria.

"You're in trouble, you're in trouble," one girl sing-songed.

"I didn't know big girls got sent to the principal's office," said the other. Ellie threw them a dirty look. Ellie McKelvey *didn't* get sent to the principal's office.

Until today.

Ellie swung her feet back and forth, wishing the principal would hurry up. And then again, hoping she wouldn't. Who knew what happened in the principal's office? Everyone who had been there said it looked like a dungeon.

"Hey, you kicked my chair," said Victoria, voice muffled by the hanky over her nose.

"Did not," said Ellie.

"Did too. Keep your dumb old feet to yourself." She elbowed Ellie.

"Cut that out." Ellie gave her an elbow back.

"Aw, your mother wears army boots," sneered Victoria. "And your brother don't."

Ellie jumped up, fists clenched. "You take that back." *Ouch!* She glanced down to see playground cinders sticking to her bloody knees.

"Oh yeah? Says who?" Victoria's knees were bloody, too.

"Says me!"

"Oh yeah?" Victoria sprang out of her chair, dropping the hanky and grabbing a fistful of Ellie's blouse. Victoria's brown eyes narrowed with meanness.

Thwack. Thwack. Thwack. Victoria's other hand froze in midair. Behind the frosted glass door labeled MISS DEETCH, PRINCIPAL, somebody had just gotten three licks with the principal's special paddle. A bed slat, Ellie had heard, drilled with holes for greater stinging power.

Again, *thwack, thwack, thwack.* Then footsteps crossing the floor. Victoria let go of Ellie's blouse just as the door creaked open. Two boys slunk out, rubbing their backsides.

"Girls!" The principal's voice seemed to come from far away. "Into my office, please."

Ellie and Victoria slouched past Miss Deetch, into the dungeon.

Doomed, thought Ellie as the door clicked shut. At least we won't get paddled. Only boys got The Paddle. But then girls didn't get sent to the office, either. Especially not sixth-grade ones.

Miss Deetch seated herself at a desk the size of a battleship. Sunlight caught something sparkly on her dress lapel. A rhinestone eagle, with an American flag in its beak. Ellie had seen Miss Deetch every weekday since kindergarten: in the schoolyard, in assembly, standing in the front hall at dismissal. In all those years, she had never seen her wear any kind of jewelry, let alone something as big and gaudy as this pin.

The principal did not ask the girls to sit. Trying not to stare at the flashing red, white, and blue rhinestones on Miss Deetch's chest, Ellie focused on the rug beneath her saddle shoes. Under the cool and tidy demeanor of the woman across the desk, she felt rumpled and sweaty. Miss Deetch, she was quite sure, never sweated.

"Well, girls, this is not an auspicious beginning to the school year. What do you have to say for yourselves?" Without waiting for an answer, Miss Deetch forged on. "Girls fighting on the playground! And sixth graders at that! It's disgraceful—certainly not what I expect from young ladies."

Miss Deetch seemed to be talking to the air over their heads, so Ellie felt safe to look around. No whips. No shackles. No thumbscrews. The office smelled like mothballs and dusty books.

". . . McKelveys and Gandecks have gone to school here for generations . . ."

Ellie wished that Miss Deetch would just get to the point and tell them their punishment.

". . . never a moment's trouble. Good, conscientious students . . ."

Ellie shifted her weight from one foot to the other, and hoped she was missing arithmetic. She glanced up. Now Miss Deetch was talking to her hands, steepled before her on the desk.

". . . and you, Victoria. Four brothers in the service . . ."

Victoria sighed, and Ellie felt a flash of sympathy. She could tell Victoria didn't like being compared to her brothers any more than Ellie liked being compared to her sister, Sal, and Jimmy. Then she remembered—Victoria was her enemy.

"Now to the facts of the matter," Miss Deetch said, looking at the girls. "Who started this?"

"She did!" both girls shouted, pointing to each other.

"Moderate voices, please. And one at a time. Victoria?"

"She hit me first. Punched me right in the nose."

"Eleanor?" Miss Deetch raised her eyebrows. "Is this true?"

"Yes, ma'am. But she called my brother Jimmy a slacker."

"Well he *is* a slacker!" huffed Victoria. "I don't see a uniform on him."

"He has a deferment." To Miss Deetch, Ellie explained, "On account of Pop breaking his leg last winter, so he couldn't walk his mail route. Jimmy was the only one working at our house, so he couldn't get drafted. He's no slacker."

"Your pop's been back at work for months," said Victoria. "Jimmy's a slacker, all right. And me with four brothers in the service. Frankie and Buddy and Hal and George. Buddy and Hal are in the Pacific and George is . . ."

"That is enough, Victoria," said Miss Deetch. Ellie snickered to herself. Once Victoria got going on her glorious brothers, all Marines, there was no shutting her up.

Miss Deetch peered over the top of her spectacles. "Let President Roosevelt and the War Department worry about Eleanor's brother."

"But she *hit* me," Victoria whined. "First."

"Yes, and it looks like *she* got the worst of it." Miss Deetch's thin lips twitched in an almost-smile. "Victoria, you were wrong to say such a thing."

Ellie shot a so-there look at Victoria. Victoria scowled.

"But Eleanor, you were equally wrong in striking her. 'A soft answer turneth away wrath,' it says in the Bible. And you, Victoria." Miss Deetch leveled a look her way. "The Bible also says that you should turn the other cheek."

"Yes, ma'am, but then my other cheek would've gotten smacked, too," Victoria protested.

"Victoria Gandeck!" roared Miss Deetch. "Holy Scripture is not to be made light of."

"Yes, ma'am." Victoria bowed her head. You don't fool me, thought Ellie.

Miss Deetch rose from her chair. "Girls, shake hands and apologize."

"Is that all?" Victoria blurted out. "Ma'am," she added hastily.

Miss Deetch twitched her almost-smile again.

"There's enough fighting in the world. We must think before we strike." The principal fingered the eagle brooch. "You are two of a kind, Eleanor and Victoria."

"What?" said both girls, forgetting to use their moderate voices.

This time Miss Deetch actually smiled. "What I mean is that you are both proud of your brothers."

"Humph," grunted Victoria. "She can keep her old slack . . . brother. *My* brothers are heroes."

"And my brother is right here, not off in some jungle fighting the Japanese," said Ellie.

Miss Deetch sighed. "I would say you two should avoid each other, but you are neighbors," she said.

"Yes, ma'am," Ellie volunteered. "Across-the-alley neighbors." She twiddled her skirt hem, and noticed it was torn.

"Then shake hands, and apologize," said the principal, coming from behind her desk.

The girls touched hands quickly and mumbled "Sorry."

"Very good," said Miss Deetch. "Now go to the washroom and clean up before you go back to class. We don't want to give Miss Granberry a fright."

Victoria beat a hasty exit out the frosted-glass door. Ellie started to follow, but Miss Deetch held up a hand.

"One at a time, Eleanor."

Alone with the principal, Ellie tried not to squirm. The room hummed with quiet, so Ellie said the first thing that came to mind.

"That's a nice pin you're wearing, Miss Deetch."

Miss Deetch continued to look at her.

"It's real patriotic and . . . and . . ."

"Thank you, Eleanor." But Miss Deetch's chin quivered, eyes blinking rapidly. Ellie realized, to her horror, that the principal was about to cry.

"Did I say something wrong, Miss Deetch?" she asked. "I'm sorry."

The principal cleared her throat and forced a smile. "It's not your fault, my dear. The pin was a gift from my nephew in the service."

"Oh," said Ellie. "Where is he now?" As soon as she said it, she wished she hadn't.

"He's a prisoner of the Japanese. We do not know exactly where. We haven't had word in some while." She stroked the brooch. "Cherish this time with your brother, Eleanor. You don't know when he'll be called into the service."

Miss Deetch squared her shoulders, and in her usual principal's voice said, "Run along and wash up now. And no dillydallying on the way to class."

Ellie scuttled off to the girl's washroom, still arguing in her head with Miss Deetch.

You're wrong, Miss Deetch. By now, the draft board has forgotten all about Jimmy.

But even to Ellie, her thoughts sounded as hollow as the feeling in her stomach.

2

Ellie had not missed arithmetic after all. And Miss Granberry did not forget the unfinished homework.

"Eleanor, please remain in your seat," she said when class was dismissed for the day.

Ellie's best friend, Stan Kozelle, shot her a sympathetic look on his way out the door. Victoria gave her a look, too. One that said, "Ha ha, you're staying after school on a Friday."

Miss Granberry marched down the aisle like Grim Death in her rusty, black sateen dress. Though shorter than most of her students, she was not a person to trifle with.

"Eleanor, I expect homework to be done at home. If not, you will do it here, after school." Miss Granberry didn't sound mad. She sounded matter-of-fact.

Ellie didn't feel matter-of-fact at all. She thumped open her arithmetic book and tried to focus on the endless rows of long-division problems. Through the open window, she heard the *ka-chung ka-chung* of skates on concrete. Who still had a pair of skates? Everyone Ellie knew had given theirs to the Junior Commandos' scrap metal drive.

Erase, erase, erase. Ellie blew eraser crumbs from her paper, wishing the answers would magically appear.

They didn't.

Out on the playground, a softball game was in progress. Every inch of Ellie longed to be out there, running bases in the afternoon sun.

"Hey batter batter batter." Victoria's outfield chatter didn't help Ellie's mood. Perfect arithmetic papers marched across the bulletin board, each with a red 100 and a gold paper star. Four of those papers had Victoria's name at the top. Ellie gritted her teeth and burrowed into the next row of problems. At last, Ellie dropped the much-erased assignment on Miss Granberry's desk.

"Thank you, Eleanor," said the teacher. "Have a pleasant weekend."

"Yes, ma'am. You, too." Ellie scuttled down the silent hallway. A small flag with a blue star fluttered on Mrs. Miller's fourth-grade door as she passed. Mrs. Miller's husband was in the Navy.

At the top of the stairs Ellie eyed the broad banister, the shiny, varnished wood. Jimmy told her he had slid down that banister once . . . and smack into Miss Deetch.

"What'd she say?" Ellie had asked.

Jimmy chuckled. "She said, 'James McKelvey, whatever possessed you?' "

"And you said . . . ?" Ellie prompted.

" 'Beg pardon, Miss Deetch. But sometimes you have to let the joy out.' "

Joyful was not how Ellie felt after spending the better part of Friday afternoon in school. An escaped convict was more like it, a fugitive from Miss Granberry's chain gang. She bounded down the steps two at a time, landing with a thud at the bottom and face-to-face with the War Bond poster next to the principal's office. A Jap soldier with an evil smile aimed a bayonet straight at Ellie. DEFEAT THE ENEMY, screamed the blood-red lettering. BUY WAR BONDS AND STAMPS.

The poster always made Ellie wonder. The only Japanese people she knew had run the game stands at West View Park. Small, gentle folks, who talked little, but smiled when a child won a Kewpie doll or a West View pennant. They went away every fall, when the park closed, and reappeared in the spring. Ellie imagined that, like the birds, the park people went south for the winter. But that first spring after Pearl Harbor, they hadn't returned. Now, high school boys ran the Ring Toss and Shooting Gallery. What happened to the Japanese? Could they, those quiet people at West View, be the enemy, like the poster soldier? When did they become *Japs*?

It's Friday, Ellie scolded herself. Time's awastin'.

Outside, the ballgame was already over, the schoolyard deserted. After four, Ellie guessed from the shadows slanting across the asphalt. The sky still blared a clear, hot blue, unusual for the North Side. It didn't take much for the steel-mill smoke from the South Side to blow their way, darkening the sky even on the sunniest of days.

Ellie trudged up Macken Street. Past the Jelineks' house with the peeling paint. The Hales', who owned the butcher shop. Past the Schmidts' tidy brick with crayon-colored flower beds. The green-shingled Gandeck house, across the alley from Ellie's. Service flags, like the one on the fourth grade's door, hung in many doors and windows.

"A star for each family member in the service," Jimmy had told her when they first appeared after Pearl Harbor. "Blue for the living. Gold for the dead."

A blue star in the Jelineks' window. Four blue stars on the Gandecks' front door. Gold on the Schmidts'. Japs had torpedoed Bill Schmidt's ship. When she first saw the gold stars, Ellie had decided they were bad luck. Now she crossed her fingers and spit in the gutter, taking the curse off Bill's gold star.

Coming to her own house, Ellie spied the loaded clothesline in the backyard. Everybody else did wash on Mondays, but not Mom. "Why would I ruin the start of a week by doing the wash?" she always said. Right this minute, she was probably in the cellar, running the wringer or ironing, and listening to the portable radio.

Ellie poked a cautious head through the back door.

"Mom?" Cans of salmon and peas on the countertop, noodles boiling on the stove. Ellie knew what that meant—salmon pea wiggle for supper—ick.

From the cellar, a tenor warbled a love song. "Down here," Mom's voice came back faintly.

"I'm home," Ellie shouted over the *thump-thump-thump* of the washer and "Indian Love Call." She peeked in the hallway. Empty. Good. If Sal were home, she would be sprawled on the floor of the phone nook, yakking on the phone to one of her birdbrain friends. Late as it was, Ellie thought Sal might have beaten her home from high school.

Ellie ran upstairs, unzipping her skirt en route. She stuffed it under her bed until she could fix the hem, hoping Sal wouldn't find it. Sal would be sure to snitch on her to Mom, just for meanness.

But then Sal pretended Ellie's half of the room didn't exist. Sal's bureau top held April Showers talcum powder, her pink celluloid dresser set—comb, brush, mirror—and a pink-framed picture of Frank Sinatra, all arranged just so.

Ellie's bureau top was a tangle of school papers, marbles, and baseball cards. In the corner of the mirror frame, she had tucked the card of her favorite player, Arky Vaughan.

"Traitor," she said to Arky's handsome cardboard face as she dug through the drawers for play clothes. Ellie would never get over him leaving the Pittsburgh Pirates, traded to the Brooklyn Dodgers. In her opinion, Arky should've quit baseball, rather than play for the rotten old Dodgers.

Baseball season was not the same without Arky belting homers into the stands of Forbes Field.

As she changed into dungarees and a jersey, Ellie caught sight of herself in the mirror, just to the left of Arky. That red blotch would be a blazing black eye by this time tomorrow.

She tied her sneakers and galloped downstairs. Pop would be home soon from the post office. She didn't want to run into him just now. But she knew that sooner or later she would have to explain this to her folks. Maybe she'd tell them she got hit by a softball.

"Mom, I'm going to Stan's," she yelled from the cellar steps. She breathed in the sudsy smell of Rinso, along with the spidery mustiness of the basement.

"Fine, dear," said Mom. "Don't forget to meet Jimmy's streetcar." Jimmy worked at Kaufmann's, the big department store Downtown, and took the Number 10 streetcar to and from work.

"Don't I always?" And I always will, thought Ellie with determination. So what if there is a war? It's a million trillion miles away from Pittsburgh and Macken Street. And Jimmy and me.

But as she crossed the street to the Kozelles', Miss Deetch's voice interrupted her thoughts. *Cherish this time with your brother, Eleanor. You don't know when he'll be called into the service.*

Ellie shivered, and tried to forget Miss Deetch's words as she hopped up Stan's front steps. She punched shave-

and-a-haircut-two-bits on the doorbell. The Kozelles had a modern push-button bell, unlike the McKelveys' old-fashioned twirling bell handle.

"Keep your shirt on," Stan shouted from somewhere beyond the screen door. His grinning face appeared from behind the mesh. "You don't look bad for somebody who got pasted by Victoria Gandeck," he added, opening the door.

"*I* got pasted?" Ellie gave Stan a playful shove. "Did she say that? The big liar!"

Stan shoved her back. "Yeah, she said that. What I don't get is why a shrimp like you would pick a fight with Victoria in the first place."

"Shrimp?" Ellie pretended to be insulted. "Look who's talking."

"Are you saying I'm *small*?" Stan fake-sneered back. They broke up laughing. Stan wasn't the smallest boy in the class. That was Oscar Jelinek, aka Jellyneck. Nor was he the biggest. That was Ralph Stankavitch, who had been left back so many times he was the only sixth grader who shaved.

No, Stan was a middle-sized boy, with freckles, a friendly, beaver-toothed smile, and spectacles that he was supposed to wear and mostly didn't.

"How'm I ever going to be a pilot, wearing specs?" he'd gripe. "I'm training my eyes to be stronger."

"Train them elsewhere," said Miss Granberry. "I expect you to see the blackboard."

This afternoon, Stan wasn't wearing his glasses. Again.

"Wanna play Monopoly?" he asked, reaching for the game in the hall closet.

"Only if you wear your specs. I get tired of reading the cards to you."

"Oh, all right." Stan handed Ellie the box as he fished the glasses from his shirt pocket.

Mrs. Kozelle clicked into the living room in her spectator pumps, and snapped on the radio. "Time for my story," she said, settling into an armchair with a knitting bag. "I always listen while supper is in the oven," she added, as if apologizing for sitting down in her own house.

I'm never going to be a housewife, thought Ellie. Nothing but work, work, work!

"And now," the announcer's voice oozed, "it's time for the trials and tribulations of *Back Stage Wife*." An organist hit an ominous chord, followed by a fancy arpeggio.

Stan rolled his eyes. "Too hot to play in here, anyway. Let's go outside."

The two friends set up the game on the front porch floor, the chill of slick cement seeping through Ellie's worn dungarees.

"So really, why did you get into it with Victoria?" Stan counted out the Monopoly money.

"She called Jimmy a slacker. I wasn't gonna let her get away with that."

Stan sorted the property cards without looking at Ellie.

"Well, aren't you gonna say something?" she demanded. "I was right, wasn't I?"

"I guess," said Stan. "But I bet he gets called slacker by adults all the time."

Ellie counted out the play money. "Why would they care if Jimmy's in the service or not?"

"It burns folks up to see someone like him safe at home, when their relatives are getting shot at. But Jimmy'll probably get drafted now that your dad is back at work."

"Maybe. Maybe not." Her stomach had that hollow feeling again.

They played a few turns in silence. Finally Stan said, "What's with you? You're acting all squirrelly."

"Nothing's with me," Ellie snapped. "I want to buy Marvin Gardens."

Stan flipped her the deed card. "You know what I think?"

"I don't care and it's your turn."

"I think you don't want Jimmy to go to war. And I'm going to buy Park Place."

"So what if I don't?" Ellie said, rolling the dice.

"Everybody's going." Stan pushed up his glasses. "The Army drafted my cousin Arnold and he's got a wife, two kids, and flat feet. If they took him, they'll take anybody." He squinted at the game board. "You owe me thirty-five dollars for landing on Park Place."

"And I've got doubles," she said, grabbing the dice and rolling. "Maybe the draft board doesn't know Pop's back at work."

"Sure they know. If Jimmy didn't tell them, he'd be in trouble. Going-to-jail kind of trouble."

"Jail? Really?" Ellie gulped. "Golly, I never thought of that."

Ellie passed Go and Stan handed her two hundred dollars.

"Yeah, jail," Stan said. "You're nuts. I wish I had a brother who was going to go bomb the bejeebers out of the Japs." He passed Go and collected his own two hundred.

"Stanley!" Mrs. Kozelle shouted from the living room.

"Sorry, Ma," he yelled. Then to Ellie, "Don't you want Jimmy to be a hero?"

"No!" Ellie shook the dice and let them fly. They bounced off the game board and rolled under the porch glider. "What if he gets killed?"

Stan retrieved the dice. "People we know don't get killed."

"Bill Schmidt got killed," Ellie pointed out.

"Yeah, but we didn't really *know* Bill. Not like we know Jimmy."

Stan had a point. The only person Ellie knew who had died was Grandpop McKelvey, and he had been very old.

"I still don't want him to go." A softball-size lump lodged in Ellie's throat. Only Jimmy thought she was smart and funny and as beautiful as Lana Turner, the movie star.

Stan jiggled the dice in his hand. "I wouldn't go around saying that, if I were you. People might get the idea you're unpatriotic."

"Me? Unpatriotic? I buy war stamps. I collect metal for scrap drives."

"I don't mean that kind of stuff." Stan sounded solemn. "Look at all the kids we know with somebody in the war. We all must make our sacrifices."

"You sound like Miss Granberry." Meatless days and giving your skates to the scrap drive were sacrifices. People shouldn't be sacrifices.

But she could never tell anyone how she felt. No one would understand, not even her best friend.

Right now, that best friend was staring over her shoulder with a funny look. Ellie followed his gaze to the sidewalk.

"It's just Sal," she said with disgust.

"Hey, Peanut," Sal called. "Better get home and set the table. It's your turn."

"Is not. It's your turn," Ellie hollered. "And don't call me Peanut." But Sal was already out of earshot, skirt sashaying, red-gold curls catching the sun.

St. Matthew's carillon tolled the hour, then played a hymn as it did every evening at six. "Rock of Ages" tonight. Time for Jimmy's streetcar.

"Gotta go, pal." Ellie swiped the game pieces into the Monopoly box.

"How come we never finish a game?" Stan said.

"Beats me," said Ellie, jumping off the porch steps. "Next time, okay?"

The trees cast long shadows across the still-warm sidewalks as late afternoon became early evening. Delicious smells tickled Ellie's nose. Creosote oozing from telephone poles. Asphalt bubbling around the trolley tracks. Supper cooking in a dozen different kitchens. Familiar, happy smells. Ignoring her sore knees, Ellie hopped through an abandoned hopscotch court on her way to the car stop.

Because this was the very best time of the day.

When Jimmy came home from work.

3

"Pardon me, boy, is that the Chattanooga Choo-Choo?" The jukebox music drifted through the screen door at Green's Soda Fountain.

"Pardon me, boy, is that the Number 10 trolley?" Ellie crowded her own words into the song. "Friday is payday, best day of the week."

Payday used to mean little surprises for Ellie from Jimmy: a roll of Lifesavers or a pack of Clark's Teaberry gum. But those things disappeared with the war and sugar rationing. Payday now meant Saturday night movies with Jimmy. Ellie could happily spend the afternoon at the Liberty with Stan and the rest of the neighborhood kids, go home for supper, then return with Jimmy to see the same movie at the evening show.

She squinted at the Liberty marquee, two blocks away. *Somewhere I'll Find You* starring Clark Gable and Lana Turner. Lana Turner. Jimmy would want to see that.

Rumble-rattle-click. Ellie turned in time to see the Number 10 screech to a stop, and the door clank open. Jimmy jumped from the top step, jacket over his arm, a rolled *Sun-Telegraph* in hand. Behind him, Victoria's father, Mr. Gandeck, lumbered off, mopping his broad face with a hanky.

"Hi there, Movie Star," said Jimmy, giving Ellie a one-armed hug. He smelled like Vitalis hair tonic, Mennen aftershave, and Downtown grit. A Jimmy sort of smell.

"Hello, girlie," said Mr. Gandeck. He fanned himself with his copy of the *Telegraph.* "Hot enough for you? How's tricks in the sixth grade?"

"Okay." Ellie looked away, keeping her bruised eye out of sight.

Mr. Gandeck socked Jimmy in the shoulder in a friendly way. "I'm gonna wet my whistle before I go home. Care to join me?" He waved a hammy hand toward the Do-Drop-Inn Tavern, across from Green's.

"No, thanks," said Jimmy, jingling the change in his pocket. "Mom doesn't like to wait supper." Most of the neighborhood men stopped for a beer on the way home, but not Jimmy or Pop.

"Suit yourself," said Mr. Gandeck. "It's too hot to go home without a beer or two." He plodded across the street as the streetcar rattled off around the corner.

"A beer or three or six." Jimmy winked at Ellie. "If I was married to Mrs. Gandeck, I might need a beer or two myself. Can that lady yell!"

"And how!" Ellie agreed. In open-window weather, the

McKelveys heard more of the Gandecks' business than they cared to.

Ellie tucked her hand into the crook of her brother's arm. It really was too hot to be so close. But if she held on, maybe he wouldn't go away.

"Looks like the Liberty is showing a Lana picture," Jimmy said. "Got any plans for Saturday night?"

"Nope." Ellie grinned up at her brother. Jimmy stopped short, shaking off her hand.

"Let's see that face." He cupped her chin in his hand. "That wouldn't be a black eye, would it?"

"Um, I guess," mumbled Ellie, wrenching free.

"Have you been in a fight?" Jimmy sounded like Pop.

"I guess." She kicked a rock, sending it across the trolley tracks.

"What do you mean, you *guess*? Either you were, or you weren't." Jimmy held her by the shoulders, forcing her to look at him. "Who with?"

"Victoria," Ellie admitted.

"Are you nuts? Victoria's as big as a Frigidaire. Why'd you fight *her*?"

Ellie took a deep breath. "She called you a slacker."

Jimmy's stern expression vanished. "And you had to defend my honor as a patriotic American, is that it?" He laughed and slapped his thigh with the rolled-up *Telegraph*.

"It's not funny," said Ellie, a little hurt. Then she caught something in his laugh, a hard, almost bitter sound. Not like Jimmy at all.

"You can tell Victoria your brother won't be slacking much longer. Now, let's get a move on. Mom wants us to stop at Hales'." Jimmy strode off toward the butcher's, Ellie galloping after him.

"You mean you told the draft board about Pop?" Ellie panted as she struggled to keep up with Jimmy's long stride.

"Of course I did, kiddo," said Jimmy. "It's the law."

"Maybe they don't need soldiers so awful bad." Ellie suggested. "You should see Miss Granberry's bulletin board."

"Miss Granberry?" Jimmy sounded puzzled, but like himself again.

"She's got photos of her old students in the service tacked to the bulletin board. Must be a hundred of 'em, at least."

"At least." Jimmy's hard-soled work shoes made a crisp, grownup sound on the pavement, Ellie's tennis shoes softly slapping on the offbeat. "She's been teaching since Moses was in Sunday School. I thought she retired."

"She did," said Ellie. "But a lot of teachers went to the war plants. So they called back the old teachers that aren't dead, though Miss Granberry just about is."

"She taught Sal and me. Pop, too," said Jimmy. "For all I know, she might've taught Grandpop McKelvey." He smiled. "I like that."

"What? That she's been teaching a million years?"

"No. Her students on the bulletin board. Wherever they are, they're still with Miss Granberry in Room Seven." Jimmy paused. "Do me a favor?"

"Sure."

"When I go away . . ."

"But you aren't going away," Ellie protested.

Jimmy squeezed her shoulder. "All right, *if* I go away, will you put my picture on Miss Granberry's wall? A picture of me in uniform? I want to be there with all the rest."

Ellie nodded.

"Shake on it? I've never known you to go back on a handshake."

Ellie shook.

"Why so glum, chum?" Jimmy looped a casual arm around her neck. "Not everyone is Gary Cooper, mowing down hundreds of Germans single-handed. That's just in the movies. I could wind up in a nice, boring job. Making soup or doing the payroll. Washing jeeps. They might not even give me a gun."

Ellie grinned. He was right. Somebody had to work in the office, cook the food.

"There's no telling where I'll land. Army, Navy, the Marines, who knows?" Jimmy said.

"Victoria's brothers knew they were Marines before they left home," she said.

"The Gandecks volunteered for the Marines," Jimmy said. "When Uncle Sam drafts you, you're sent wherever you're needed most."

"Oh." Ellie gulped. Between the newsreels at the Liberty and Victoria's bragging, Ellie knew the Marines were the first to land in an invasion. Dear God, not the Marines!

"Here we are," said Jimmy, pushing open Hales' door. As always, Ellie did a little soft shoe in the butcher shop saw-dust, enjoying the clean, sharp smell.

"Hi," Trudy Hale called from behind the meat case. "Got your order all ready. Got them ration books, good lookin'?"

"You betcha, beautiful," said Jimmy, taking the books from his coat pocket.

Trudy tore the coupons from the books and handed them back. Did Ellie imagine it, or did Jimmy's fingers linger longer than necessary in Trudy's hand? Jimmy called every female "beautiful," even Ruthie Green, who was as plain as a mud fence. Ellie knew he was kidding. After all, he never called any of *them* "Movie Star." But the way he looked at Trudy . . . this was different.

Ellie thought he might say more, but just then, Mrs. Gandeck blew through the door.

"Hear you have brisket today," she hollered before the door banged behind her. "Give me what you've got." Catching sight of Jimmy, she added. "Jim McKelvey, was Mr. Gandeck on your streetcar this evening?"

"Yes, ma'am," said Jimmy, winking at Ellie and Trudy. "I think he stopped somewhere on the way home."

Mrs. Gandeck scowled. "I'll just bet he did!" Then she caught sight of Ellie's face. "Where did you get that black eye, young lady? Funny thing, my Victoria came home with one too."

"Is that so?" Jimmy scooped the paper-wrapped meat from the counter and nudged Ellie toward the door. "Be seeing you, Trudy," he called.

"Be seeing you, handsome," Trudy called back.

"Poor Mr. Gandeck," said Jimmy. "It's going to be loud across the alley tonight."

"Yeah," said Ellie. But her mind wasn't on their noisy neighbors. "Is Trudy your girlfriend?"

Jimmy considered for a moment. "If I had a girlfriend, it would be Trudy. But girlfriends take time and money, and I don't have much of either. And if I *do* go in the service, it wouldn't be fair to tie a girl to me. For now, you're my best girl."

Good! Ellie thought. I don't have to share him with anybody. At least not yet.

Jimmy grabbed Ellie's hand and burst into "The Hut-Sut Song." She quickly scanned the block to see if anyone was around to hear. It was one thing for the King Sisters to sing "Hut-Sut Rawlson on the rillerah" on the radio, and quite another for your big brother to do it on Macken Street in broad daylight.

"Sing," Jimmy urged. "Let the joy out."

"Why can't you let it out where people can't see or hear you?" Ellie said.

Jimmy dropped her hand. "Gee, Movie Star, life's too short not to be happy."

Ellie shot him a look.

"All right, all right," he said with a sigh. "I'll be joyful when you're not around, okay?"

"Okay." Ellie squeezed his hand. They both said, "No hard feelings?" Then, laughing, "Owe you a nickel," as they did whenever they said the same thing at the same time.

Jimmy picked up his pace. "Shake a leg, girl. I'm hungry."

Ellie shook a leg, and once again tried to keep up with her brother's long legs. At the terrace steps that led from the sidewalk up the steeply sloped lawn, Jimmy paused and sniffed the air. "Salmon pea wiggle?"

"Yep," said Ellie, wrinkling her nose.

Jimmy laughed. "Hey, kiddo, don't you know there's a war on?" He took the steps two at a time. "Hurry up." He banged through the screen door as Mom yelled, "Will you kids stop banging that screen door?"

Ellie paused at the mailbox; she could see envelopes through the mail slot. She twirled the lock and lifted the lid. Three letters. One from Gramma Guilfoyle in West Virginia. One from Aunt Toots, Mom's youngest sister, who lived with Gramma. And one envelope addressed to Mr. James Armstrong McKelvey. From Selective Service. *Official Business.*

The draft board.

Her stomach nosedived, the way it did on the Dips at West View Park.

Inside, Jimmy called, "Mom, I'm starving. When's supper?"

"Sally Jane, get off that telephone *now*!" Mom yelled. Pot lids clattered and a drawer slammed. "I need help in the kitchen."

"Upside down, inside out, this house is like a three-ring circus," Pop shouted over his news program. "Can't a man have some peace and quiet? Sal, help your mom lift supper to the table."

Ellie slumped against the porch glider, listening to the familiar suppertime noises.

She put the letters back in the box, took a deep breath, and went inside.

That night, Ellie lay in bed, watching the dotted swiss curtains breathe in and out of the windows in the autumn-tinged breeze.

Downstairs, she could hear the laughter of a radio show audience. Bob Hope, probably. She smelled the pungent remains of salmon pea wiggle.

Across the alley, Mr. Gandeck's accordion wheezed out "Oh Marie." When the Gandecks had a fight, Mr. Gandeck played "Oh Marie" because that was Mrs. Gandeck's name. Ellie wished they'd make up so she could go to sleep.

Go to sleep and pretend that things would always be the same . . . Bob Hope and salmon pea wiggle and "Oh Marie." Seeing Lana Turner pictures with Jimmy at the Liberty.

Pretend that there wasn't a letter in the mailbox for Mr. James Armstrong McKelvey, from Selective Service.

Official Business.

4

BY ORDER OF THE PRESIDENT OF THE UNITED STATES,
JAMES ARMSTRONG MCKELVEY IS TO REPORT TO UNION
STATION AT 6 A.M. ON THE DAY OF OCTOBER 2, 1943.

Ellie counted the days on the kitchen calendar. October 2 was a Saturday. Twenty-one days until Jimmy had to go. That was a long time. Maybe the war would be over by then.

But the days slipped by as fast as the trees shed their leaves. And the war didn't end.

The Saturday before he left, dozens of Jimmy's friends came by the house to wish him well. High school friends. Friends from the neighborhood. Friends from work. Some Ellie knew; some she didn't.

When it looked as though a party was going to happen, Jimmy went upstairs to change clothes. He came back wearing his Hawaiian shirt, hula girls and palm trees swaying from collar to hem. Jimmy only wore it on "special occasions."

"Hubba-hubba," Sal commented, heaving old copies of *Life* magazine into the entry closet.

Jimmy struck a pose. "Am I not the very image of Bing Crosby in *Road to Singapore?*"

Ellie smiled. "You sure it wasn't Bob Hope? He was in that movie, too." She and Sal had pooled their money to buy Jimmy that shirt for his birthday. Somehow, it just looked like Jimmy, crazy and carefree.

More people showed up, and before long, boys were rolling up the carpets and shoving furniture against the walls. Pop glowered as they pushed his Morris chair and ottoman into a corner. He pushed both right back to their spot by the radio.

"You kids want to dance, do it around me," he grumbled. "Got a bum leg, y'know."

Word spread. "Party at the McKelveys'. Jim's going in the service."

As afternoon faded to evening, neighbors arrived with food. Mrs. Gandeck bustled in with her famous pierogies, the aroma of cooked onions filling the house. Trudy Hale arrived hefting a platter of chipped ham. Meanwhile, Mom was in the kitchen, using the last of September's sugar ration and stirring up Jimmy's favorite, gingerbread with cream cheese icing.

Mr. Green brought a bucket of ice cream and his grown daughter Ruthie to scoop it.

"Howsabout a little goodbye sugar, Ruthie?" Jimmy teased.

"Jimmy McKelvey, you're the biggest kidder," said Ruthie, hugging the elbows of her mouse-gray cardigan.

"Then I'll just have to take that sugar myself." Jimmy dipped Ruthie backward, giving her a long, noisy kiss. Her ice-cream scoop clattered to the floor.

"Whoo-hoo!" hollered Mr. Gandeck. "The Army has landed!" His accordion crashed into "Roll Out the Barrel," and Jimmy swept the breathless Ruthie off in a clumsy polka.

Over and over, Ellie was asked, "Aren't you proud of your brother?" She smiled and nodded, all the while thinking, No! I don't want him to go. Finally she hid in the phone nook under the hall stairs, where she could see without being in the thick of things.

The party swirled on around Pop and his bum leg. "Yes, we're proud of him," he shouted over the music, when people stopped to talk. "General Patton better watch out for General McKelvey! Admiral Nimitz, too!" When there was a break in the well-wishing, he waved Ellie over. "Peanut, how long are these folks going to stay? *Gang Busters* comes on the radio soon."

"Beats me." Ellie shrugged. "They're having a good time."

"I wish somebody would pull the plug on Gandeck," Pop grumbled. "The only two songs he knows are 'Roll Out the Barrel' and 'Oh Marie.' "

Mr. Corsiglia, the grocer, stuck his head in the front door. "Soda pop in the ice tub out here. Get 'em while they're cold."

"Save one for me," shouted Mr. Gandeck, hoisting the accordion from his shoulders. "I'm taking a break."

"Hallelujah," said Pop. "Maybe the place will clear out."

But Jimmy was already at the record player. Glenn Miller's "Moonlight Serenade" filled the room, slow and dreamy. Someone snapped off the lights, and couples crowded the makeshift dance floor.

"That does it," said Pop, struggling to his feet. "I'm going to listen to the radio in the kitchen. At least a man can hear himself think out there." In a minute, Ellie heard the gunfire and police sirens of *Gang Busters*.

Ellie found Stan and Jellyneck in the dining room, building skyscraper sandwiches with Trudy's ham. Jellyneck looked grubbier than usual, with his dirt-streaked jersey, and socks drooping into battered tennis shoes. He pulled a chair up to the buffet table and dug into the mountain of food on his plate, ignoring folks reaching over his head for ham and potato salad. Ellie and Stan leaned against the sideboard with their food, watching the action in the living room.

"Euww." Stan waved his fork toward the dancers. "Look at 'em. Stuck together like wet leaves."

"Euww," Ellie echoed, but secretly she thought that someday, dancing with a boy might be fun. She watched Jimmy drift by with Trudy.

"She Jimmy's girlfriend?" Jellyneck asked around a mouthful of potato salad.

"No," Ellie said. But she'd share him with anybody, if only he wouldn't go away.

"Moonlight Serenade" ended, and the lights flashed on.

"Enough of that slow stuff," shouted Sal. "Pep it up!"

As Benny Goodman's "Sing, Sing, Sing" thumped through the room, Sal snared one of the high-school-age Jelineks, flinging him into a jitterbug. There were nine Jelinek brothers, and they all looked alike to Ellie. They just came in different sizes.

Sal and her partner did some fast side kicks, their feet never missing a beat.

"Wow, Sal's some dancer," said Jellyneck.

"Yeah," said Stan. "She even makes Donnie look good." He squinted. "Or is that Sam?"

Victoria sidled up to the table, soda pop in hand. Ellie eyed the bottle suspiciously. Shook-up pop was as good as a squirt gun, and sticky, to boot.

"I'll bet your brother goes in the Army," said Victoria. "That's not as good as the Marines. The Marines are real heroes." She dipped a hand into the bowl of shelled peanuts. "My brother Buddy is gonna bring me home a Jap flag."

"Zowie," said Jellyneck. "Maybe my brother Orrie can bring me one of those."

"I doubt it," said Victoria. "Not unless he's a Marine in the Pacific. *That's* where all the *real* fighting is going on."

"No," said Jellyneck, hanging his head. "He's an Army clerk at Fort Dix, New Jersey."

Victoria's smirk made the blood pound in Ellie's ears.

"You just wait, Victoria Gandeck," she snapped. "My brother will be a hero, you wait and see. Jellyneck's, too."

"Sure," said Victoria in a bored voice, and wandered off, popping peanuts in her mouth.

"I thought you didn't want Jimmy to be a hero," said Stan.

"I don't," Ellie snapped.

"Don't bite my head off." Stan took a step back. "You're acting all squirrelly again."

"I guess you'd know about squirrels, because you're nuts," Ellie retorted. She might have said more, if Mr. Gandeck hadn't banged through the door announcing, "I'm back."

"Hey, Gandeck, play 'Roll Out the Barrel' again," someone yelled.

So he did. Again and again. *Roll out the barrel, we'll have a barrel of fun.*

Ellie retreated to the phone nook, too pooped to fight with Victoria, Stan, or anyone else. She tried not to think about where Jimmy would be this time next week. *Not the Marines, dear God,* she prayed. Anything but the Marines. The Marines got in all the big action, just as Victoria said. The big dangerous action.

The washtub on the porch held only melting ice. The ham platter and potato salad bowl were scraped clean, but the party roared on. Mr. Gandeck and his accordion had long since staggered home, but Sal kept the record player going with the loudest, fastest dance numbers she could find. The house vibrated with music and dancing and the feeling of time standing still.

Ellie winked and blinked, willing herself to stay awake. Wanting this to last forever. Everyone together, happy, safe, and the war far, far away.

The dancers blurred, the music filled Ellie's head, crowding out thought. Then the voices and melodies faded to a pleasant hum.

She fell asleep.

The music still played in Ellie's mind as she sat in church the next morning.

"Let's open our hymnals and sing Number 100," Reverend Schuyler commanded. The organist hit the opening chords of "Joyful, Joyful, We Adore Thee," banishing all thoughts of "Roll Out the Barrel."

Jimmy rolled his eyes and whispered, "Pep it up, why can't she? What is this, a funeral?"

Ellie stifled a snicker that turned into a snort. Mom leaned past Sal and Jimmy to mouth, "Be a lady." Jimmy, of course, looked perfectly innocent as he let loose on "Joyful, Joyful."

After seven verses, and an eternity, Reverend Schuyler motioned for everyone to sit.

A scrap of paper and stubby pencil landed in Ellie's lap.

Tic-tac-toe during Reverend Schuyler's endless sermons was an Ellie-and-Jimmy tradition, easy to do since Mom and Ellie sat at opposite ends of the pew.

She scratched an X as she gazed sideways at her brother and thought, *Dear God, please keep him safe. If you do, I'll pay attention in church for the rest of my life.*

Sundaymondaytuesdaywednesday. Ellie's days flew by that last week, like a speeded-up movie. She tried to hold on to each minute. This is the last time Jimmy will eat meatloaf with us. The last time he'll buy me a nickel pop at Green's. No, not *the* last time. Just until the war is over.

And then it was Friday, October 1. The *last* Friday. Ellie waited for Jimmy at the car stop. Frank Sinatra's velvety voice floated through Green's screen door. "I'll Never Smile Again." The softball lump rose in Ellie's throat.

Cut it out! It was just a dumb song. Nothing had changed, yet. They'd walk home together and talk, just like always. And maybe, just maybe, Jimmy would say something special. Something that would take away the worry that had gnawed at Ellie ever since The Letter had arrived.

The Number 10 ground to a halt, the door screeching open.

"Good luck, young fella," the gray-haired motorman called as Jimmy got off. "See you after the war."

"You betcha," Jimmy said with a farewell wave. Then, to Ellie, "Hey, Movie Star, guess who I found Downtown?"

"Mr. Gandeck?" Ellie guessed as their neighbor appeared in the trolley door. Then she noticed Jimmy carried a scuffed valise.

"So long, Jim," called Mr. Gandeck with a sloppy salute. "Kick Hitler in the heinie for me." He headed toward the Do-Drop.

"Howdy, Small Fry," a female voice boomed. Ellie looked up to see a younger, thinner version of Mom spring from the steps, lugging a giant hatbox. That is, if Mom had a frizzy permanent wave and wore saddle shoes.

"What's the matter? Dontcha know your own aunt?" The girl clapped Ellie on the back. Ellie reeled from the overpowering scent of Evening in Paris.

"Aunt Toots?" It had been a while since Ellie had seen Mom's sister. Toots was younger than Jimmy, but older than Sal. "Have you come for a visit?"

"Better'n that." Toots nudged her and winked. "I've come to stay."

"Stay?" Ellie repeated blankly.

"You betchyer boots. The whole world was doing their bit for the war, so I said to myself 'Toots, old girl, do you want to spend the war working at a five-and-dime in Lost Gap, West Virginia?' "

"You did?" Ellie couldn't figure out where the conversation was going.

"You betcha. I thought, where can I do the most good for my country?" Toots paused, as if waiting for Ellie to answer. "At a war plant, that's where, right here in Pittsburgh. And when I heard there was going to be a room to spare at your house, I knew it was meant to be. So I caught me a choo-choo, Jimmy met me at the station, and here I am."

"You're staying in Jimmy's room?" Suddenly Ellie felt dizzy, and it wasn't just from all that Evening in Paris.

"Yep. Say, sitting on my suitcase for five hours on a jam-packed train made me hungry. Let's go put on the feed bag."

Toots and Jimmy headed up Macken Street, Toots yakking away. Ellie trailed behind, firing furious, evil thoughts to the back of her aunt's head. This was Ellie's special time with Jimmy, not Toots's!

Jimmy must have said something funny because Aunt Toots stopped in her tracks and laughed. A loud, honking laugh that made Ellie's teeth hurt.

"Your brother is a card, kiddo," Toots said when Ellie caught up. "He'll keep the troops in stitches."

Ellie couldn't think of anything to say that wasn't rude or disrespectful.

Toots punched Ellie's shoulder. "Cat got your tongue? You sure are quiet. Little, too. How old are you? Eight?"

"I'll be twelve next July," she said, gritting her teeth.

"Coulda fooled me," brayed Toots. "You grow 'em short here in the city," she added to Jimmy, as if Ellie were invisible.

When they reached home, Toots took the terrace steps two at a time. "I'm billy-goat hungry," she called over her shoulder, "and you two are just poking along."

"Billy-goat hungry?" Ellie couldn't resist asking.

"Yep. So starved I could eat tin cans. Get it?" Toots and her honking laugh disappeared into the house.

Ellie turned to Jimmy. "Did you know about this? I mean, before today?"

Jimmy nodded, looking a little sheepish. "Yeah. Remember the day I got my induction notice? There were letters from Gramma and Toots that same day, asking if when I go in the service, Toots could come up and stay with us."

Ellie glared at her brother. "You could've warned me, you know," she said.

Jimmy shrugged. "Didn't want to rub it in that I was leaving. Toots isn't so bad. She's a pretty good egg when you get to know her."

"Oh yeah, she's a barrel of laughs." Ellie tossed her braids over her shoulders with an angry head jerk. "Pittsburgh is full of boardinghouses. Why is she staying with us?"

"Grampa and Gramma would never let her live in a boardinghouse. Besides, she's a paying guest. The folks are still catching up on the bills from when Pop was sick."

Ellie sighed, all the way from the soles of her sneakers.

"C'mon, it isn't as bad as all that," said Jimmy. "As they say, it's just 'for the duration.' Besides, Toots will keep things lively around here. You'll hardly miss me."

Wrong, thought Ellie as they went inside. I miss you already.

5

Ellie awoke to the smell of waffles. And coffee, real coffee, so hard to get these days. But it was pitch black outside. Too early for breakfast.

Then she remembered.

October 2.

The luminous green hands of the alarm clock pointed to four-fifteen. Downstairs, she could hear breakfast clatter. Across the hall, Sal sang over the spattering shower.

"Girls," Mom called upstairs. "Get a move on. We have to be Downtown by six."

Half asleep, Ellie staggered to the bathroom. "Hey, songbird," she shouted, pounding on the door. "Leave some hot water."

She took her own sweet time, but finally Sal banged open the door, steam whooshing out behind her.

"All yours, Peanut," she said, rubbing her wet hair with a towel.

Leaning against the sink, Ellie turned on both taps, splashed her face, and discovered that Sal had taken all the hot water. Well, she thought, at least I'm awake now!

Swiping at the steam-fogged mirror with her pajama sleeve, Ellie peered at her reflection. For a minute, she was tempted to just run a comb through the top of her hair, without redoing her braids.

Sighing, she pulled the gum bands from her braids, then brushed and rebraided her hair. Not that it did much good. For the millionth time, Ellie wished she had Sal's naturally curly hair. She felt like a wren in a family of cardinals. When they all walked down the street together, people turned to look at Sal and Jimmy with their picture-perfect hair and toothpaste-ad smiles. Ellie could be a smudge on Sal's saddle shoe, for all anyone noticed her.

Her stomach ached. After today, they wouldn't walk down the street all together again for a long, long time. She replaced the comb and brush in the medicine chest and slammed the mirrored door. Hard. That felt good.

Back in their room, Sal stood at the closet, a dress hanger in each hand. *Her* hair, Ellie noted with disgust, was already drying in damp ringlets. The scent of Sal's April Showers talcum powder was so strong, Ellie could almost taste it.

"Didn't you hear Mom say to hurry up?" asked Ellie as she buttoned her new school dress, a red plaid. The one dress that wasn't a hand-me-down from Sal.

"I can't decide." Sal held up first one dress, then the

other. "I want to look nice. There'll be a lot of people at the station."

"You mean *boy* people." Ellie tied her velvet Sunday ribbons to her braids. "Like they're going to be looking at you." She went downstairs, leaving Sal still hypnotized by the dress hangers.

"Don't you look perky," Aunt Toots called to Ellie as she came into the warm, bright kitchen. She ladled batter into the waffle iron. "One waffle or two?"

"One." Ellie didn't know how she could eat even one. Not with that pain in her stomach and lump in her throat.

Mom poured Ellie's milk into her Captain Midnight tumbler. Pop read the morning paper, the *Post-Gazette*, as he sipped his coffee. Across the table, Jimmy shoveled in waffles as fast as he could spear them. Just like any morning.

But it wasn't any morning. Dark windows reflected a blurry, ghostly family moving about the kitchen. The ceiling light glared off the chrome toaster and breadbox. The grownups dressed in going-Downtown clothes. Only Jimmy, in an old pullover and corduroys, looked his usual Saturday self.

Pop folded the paper and frowned at his watch. "If Sal doesn't get down here pronto, she's not going to the station."

Mom shouted from the kitchen doorway, "Sal, hurry up."

Sal's saddle shoes galloped down the stairs. "I'm here,

I'm here." And wearing her church dress, Ellie observed. And lipstick. And looking a little bustier than she had ten minutes ago.

Aunt Toots dropped a waffle on Ellie's plate.

"Wow, real coffee," said Sal, sniffing noisily. "Can I have some?"

"No, you may not," said Mom. "Not until you're old enough for your own coffee ration. Now sit down and eat."

Toots plunked a plate in front of Sal.

"I'm not hungry," yawned Sal. "Good gosh, it's practically the middle of the night."

"I'll take hers," said Jimmy with his mouth full.

Any other morning, Mom would have said, "Don't talk with your mouth full." Any other morning, Mom would've noticed Sal's lipstick and told her to wipe it off.

Sal shoved her waffle toward Jimmy, then stood by the back door, admiring her reflection in the dark glass. Ellie skated her own waffle around the plate in a lake of syrup.

"Movie Star, if you aren't going to eat that, pass it over here," said Jimmy, after polishing off Sal's breakfast.

Ellie handed her plate across the table without a word.

"Don't know where my next meal is coming from," Jimmy said with a wink. "But I'll bet it's not gonna be waffles."

All too quickly, breakfast was over. Time to go.

"Leave the dishes in the sink," called Mom, putting on her Sunday hat in front of the mantel mirror. "Time enough later to do them."

Mom *never* left dishes in the sink.

Turning from the mirror, Mom surveyed Jimmy. "Why didn't you wear your good pants and jacket? Put on a tie?"

Jimmy laughed and gave Mom a hug. "The service will give me all the clothes I need for the next couple of years."

Mom wasn't pacified. "What will people think?"

But Jimmy had gone out to the porch. "Better wear your coats. It's nippy out," he reported through the open door.

Wrapped in coats and babushkas, the family stepped into the foggy darkness. How different her street looked at this hour between night and morning. Ellie shivered.

"Cold, Movie Star?" Jimmy asked.

Ellie nodded, putting her hands in her jacket pockets. But this kind of cold couldn't be fixed with gloves or mittens.

"Can't see the hand before me," Pop grumbled. "Why can't we scrape the paint off the streetlights? The Nazis aren't going to bomb Macken Street."

"You never know," said Mom. "Best to err on the side of caution."

"Well, it's a blamed nuisance," Pop said. "I don't want to break my leg again, stumbling around in the dark."

"Sissies," Aunt Toots scolded. "No streetlights a'tall where I come from. Never were, likely never will be."

Stepping cautiously, the family made their way to the streetcar stop.

Ellie crossed her fingers, hoping the streetcar would be late.

Trudy Hale was waiting for them in front of the butcher shop.

"A little something for the train," she said, handing Jimmy a string-tied Florsheim shoebox.

"Wow, shoes!" he said, dropping his suitcase. "Just what I needed."

"Oh *you*!" Trudy playfully poked Jimmy's shoulder. "It's chipped ham sandwiches, dill pickles, and molasses cookies. Eat the pickles first. They might soak through the wax paper."

"Thank you, Trudy," Mom said. "With all the commotion, I forgot to pack a lunch."

Trudy waved off the thanks. "You can't get chipped ham anywheres but Pittsburgh, you know."

"Gee, and I didn't get anything for you," said Jimmy, still in his kidding voice. "This will have to do." He pulled Trudy to him and kissed her. Not a long, romantic kiss, but not the goofing-around kind he had given Ruthie Green, either.

"Say," Sal whispered. "I didn't know Jimmy was that way about Trudy."

"He's not," Ellie whispered back.

"How do you know?" Sal whispered, louder than before.

"Cut it out, you two." Aunt Toots nudged Ellie and Sal.

Slowly, Jimmy and Trudy pulled away from each other.

"You take care now, Jimmy McKelvey," said Trudy. "Give 'em hell." Her words were teasing, but her voice was serious.

"You betcha." Jimmy picked up his suitcase. "Better get inside before you freeze."

"I suppose," said Trudy. But when they reached the car stop, Ellie looked back to see Trudy hugging herself in the pale light from the open shop door, leaves skittering at her feet.

"Trudy's still there," Ellie said.

"Wave to your sugar," Sal added in a sickly-sweet voice. Ellie shoved her. Sal shoved back. Jimmy raised a farewell hand just as the Number 10 clacked up the hill. The brightly lit, nearly empty car looked like a lightning bug in the dark.

"Today's the day, ain't it now, Jim," said the morning conductor, as he took their trolley tokens. "Won't seem right, not seeing yunz first thing of the day."

"Yes, sir," said Jimmy. "But I'll be back before you know it."

"Darn tootin'," said the conductor. "Give them Nazis a run for their money. Wish I could go myself, but not with these peepers." He pointed to his thick-lensed spectacles.

Ellie took comfort in her brother's words, and the bad feeling in her stomach eased a little. Back before you know it, is what he said.

Mom and Pop sat behind the motorman. Jimmy started to sit across from them, Sal following. Ellie slid in front of Sal. No way was Sal sitting with Jimmy this morning.

"Hey! What's the big idea?" Sal said. "I was here first."

"Says you. One more word and I'll tell Mom about the socks in your brassiere."

"No you won't!" Shove. "You little sneak!"

"Will too." Shove. "Boy-crazy."

"Girls! Stop it!" Mom shouted. The girls' mouths hung open in mid-insult. Mom shouting? In public? "Of all mornings to quarrel . . ."

"But Sal pushed me," Ellie protested.

"Tattletale," Sal snapped.

"Behave like ladies," Mom said through clenched teeth. "Or so help me I'll . . ."

"Whaddya say, Movie Star? Should we sit in our usual spot?" Jimmy suggested.

"Sure."

They made their way to their favorite seat in the rear, the long bench. A backward glance told Ellie that Sal and Aunt Toots had taken the seat across from Mom and Pop.

The trolley racketed through the silent streets as Ellie and Jimmy settled on the wicker seat. Outside, sleeping houses slipped by, a lit window here and there, the dimmed streetlamps casting pale pools of light.

"Someone else is up early," said Ellie. "Maybe they're joining the service today, too."

"Most likely they're working the weekend shift," Jimmy said. As if to prove him right, two women in overalls and babushkas, carrying lunch buckets, got on at the next stop. "Bet they work at Blaw-Knox," he added.

"Where they make radio towers?" With so many men in

the service, women did all sorts of jobs these days, but Ellie had never thought of them building radio towers.

"They switched over to war production, so who knows what they're doing," said Jimmy. "Top secret hush-hush stuff, you know."

"Oh, sure." The women didn't *look* top secret hush-hush, but you never knew.

Toots swayed down the aisle after the women and sat in front of them. She turned around and started up a quiet conversation.

"Bet she's asking if they're hiring at their plant," Jimmy said.

Clack *clack*. Clack *clack*. Clack *clack*. The last streetcar ride. Ellie stared at the advertisement rail above the windows. TIRED? NERVOUS? GET YOUR VITAMINS TODAY IN SPITE OF THE FOOD SHORTAGES. TAKE VIMMS VITAMINS!

This is stupid, Ellie realized. I should be talking, not reading ads! But what came out of her mouth was "Why do you have to go?" The tears that had threatened all week spilled over.

Jimmy pulled a clean hanky from his jacket pocket. "I had a feeling you'd need this. Now start again."

"Why do you have to go?" Ellie blew her nose. "Why can't somebody else go?"

Jimmy's eyes grew serious. "Somebody else *has* gone. Lots of somebodies. Movie stars like Clark Gable. All four of President Roosevelt's sons. Even Glenn Miller. Think of the pictures Miss Granberry has on her wall."

Ellie knew all that, but it didn't make her feel any better. "You're special."

Jimmy covered her cold hand with his warm, rough one. "Those people are special to someone, too."

Ellie just listened.

"Do I want to kill people? Hell no! If the service has to rely on my skills as a shooter, this war is in big trouble."

Ellie knew he was joking, but it wasn't funny to her. "I don't want you to get shot."

"Me either." Jimmy squeezed her hand. "I'll try to get one of those jeep-washing, paper-filing jobs."

"Promise?" asked Ellie. Jimmy always kept his promises.

"I'll do my best." He laid a hand on Ellie's babushka, like a blessing. "You know, I wouldn't be surprised if this whole thing is over by Christmas."

"Really?" Ellie counted in her head. Not quite three months. Not so terribly long.

"Why, sure." Jimmy's smile crinkled the corners of his eyes. "When Hitler hears I'm coming, he'll surrender on the spot. I won't even need a gun."

Ellie giggled. "But seriously, will you really be home for Christmas?"

Something changed in Jimmy's eyes for just a minute. Or did Ellie imagine it?

"Sure thing." No, she imagined it. "Just keep the Christmas tree up until I get there. You know how Mom chucks it out December 26."

"Sure thing," Ellie repeated. "Shake?" The tightness in

her chest eased. Jimmy never went back on a handshake promise.

The trolley bumped along the silent Saturday streets, storefronts dark and blank-faced.

"You know, Movie Star, getting drafted might be the best thing that ever happened to me. I was getting tired of all the wisecracks about fighting Hitler from Pittsburgh."

The trolley stopped, and a couple of sailors with duffel bags slung on their shoulders got on.

"I've never been anywhere except to visit Gramma and Grampa in West Virginia." Jimmy's voice now sounded dreamy. "Maybe I'll see England, like in that movie, *Mrs. Miniver*."

Ellie nodded, but Jimmy wasn't looking at her.

"Or maybe Paris, if we kick the Nazis out. I'll bet that Eiffel Tower has some view. Do you think it's taller than the Gulf Tower?"

Ellie didn't care if the Eiffel Tower was taller than the tallest building in Pittsburgh, or even the tallest building in the world.

"You act like you *want* to go!" she accused.

But Jimmy's mind was someplace else. "Or maybe an island with hula girls and coconut trees. Wonder how coconuts taste right off the tree." He sounded . . . happy.

Smothered sobs knotted in Ellie's chest. "Have a good time with your Eiffel Tower and hula girls," she said, voice shrill. "You don't care one little bit about us."

Jimmy blinked, as if he had been asleep with his eyes open. "Don't, Ellie."

"Downtown, folks," shouted the conductor. "End of the line."

"Let's go, Movie Star." Jimmy picked up his valise and Trudy's shoebox.

Ellie followed Jimmy's worn plaid jacket down the aisle. *I didn't mean it, Jimmy. I'm sorry.* But the words stuck in her throat.

Slowly, she descended the trolley steps for the two-block walk to Union Station.

Two blocks that felt like ten miles.

6

The last of the warm weather seemed to have left with Jimmy. Pop put on the storm doors and windows, banishing the screens to the basement until spring. On Monday, with the chill October winds whipping through their jackets, the sixth-graders started bringing their lunch to school so they wouldn't have to walk home in the cold. But not Ellie. She went home at noon to check the mail.

By late Tuesday, Ellie was at the end of her patience with the U.S. Post Office.

"Will you *please* stop checking the mailbox!" Sal sprawled across Pop's chair, filing her nails and listening to Frank Sinatra records. "He's only been gone three days."

"I'm not checking the mailbox," Ellie said from the porch as she quietly lifted the mailbox lid . . . again. Still empty. She came back inside. "I'm watching for Aunt Toots. To see if she found a job."

"Ha!" Sal scoffed. "Like you care. I don't know what you've got against her."

"Don't you think she's kind of, well, loud?" Ellie flopped on the couch.

"I hadn't noticed." Sal turned up the volume on the record player.

"And rude?"

Sal studied her nails. "Nah. She just tells the truth and doesn't care how it sounds."

"Well, she should." Ellie twiddled the fringe on the sofa pillow.

"You're just sore because she calls you Small Fry and Short Stuff." Sal got up to change records.

"Am not. What if we told her she stomps around like a cow, her hair looks like a Brillo pad, and she dresses like a colorblind clown?"

"Probably wouldn't bother her at all. Now, shush. This is Benny Goodman."

"Sal," Ellie yelled over Benny Goodman's wailing clarinet. "Do you think she's going to stay until the war is over?"

"Like they say," Sal shouted. "For the duration. Until the war is over."

Ellie was learning to hate those words.

Mom came to the living room arch. "For pity's sake, girls, turn down that noise."

"It's Benny Goodman, Mom," Sal said, turning the volume down slightly.

"It sounds like a cat caught in a wringer," Mom said as she left.

Benny was blasting away on "Stompin' at the Savoy," so they didn't hear Aunt Toots until she banged open the front door. "Ta-da!" she trumpeted. "I got me a job at Shiny Brite Mirrors."

"Good for you," said Mom, returning from the kitchen. "Sal, put your feet on the floor and sit like a lady, please. And turn off that so-called music!"

Sal rolled her eyes, but took Benny off the record player. "That's swell, Aunt Toots."

Ellie picked at her cuticles and thought, Now we'll *never* get rid of her.

"What kind of job is it?" Sal asked. "You aren't making mirrors, are you?"

"I can't tell you. Top secret," said Toots. "The man who hired me said 'Lady, if you can run a sewing machine, you can work here.' I didn't tell him I couldn't run a sewing machine, neither."

"Sewing machine, you say? Hmmmm." Mom's eyes had a look that Ellie knew well.

"Mom, you aren't getting a war job, are you?" she asked.

"Hey, can I get one too?" asked Sal. "Connie Cavendish, in my class, got a war job. She works the four-to-midnight shift after school."

"I don't care if Connie Cavendish shaves her head," said Mom. "You're not working an eight-hour shift in a war plant. Your job is going to school, young lady."

"But Connie Cavendish . . ." Sal went on.

". . . is not my daughter," Mom finished. "And Ellie, I'm *thinking* about a war job."

"Swell!" said Toots. "I work graveyard, so maybe you could get days. Then there'll always be someone here for the kiddos."

The "kiddos" exchanged disgusted glances.

"We can take care of ourselves," Sal grumbled.

"What's 'graveyard'?" asked Ellie. It sounded spooky.

"Night shift, eleven to seven," said Toots. "I'm gonna be a night owl. Hooty-hoot!"

"And that means you girls keep it down in the afternoon while your aunt sleeps," said Mom. "No radio. No horseplay. No fighting. No visitors unless Toots is awake and downstairs."

"But Pop gets home before five," Sal said.

"Yes, well, that might be changing, too," said Mom. "What with the war and the labor shortage, Pop might be working some evenings, too."

How swell, Ellie thought sourly. And you can bet your bottom dollar Sal is going to take her own sweet time coming home from school, so she won't have to pitch in with the chores. That's going to leave me and Toots alone in the house together.

Ellie could only hope that Toots would sleep right up until the time she left for work. Ellie was so steamed about Mom even thinking about getting a job, she forgot that Jimmy hadn't written.

At least not yet.

Wednesday. Still nothing from Jimmy.

"He's never going to write," Ellie wailed.

"Patience, Ellie," Mom said. "He'll write, you wait and see."

On Thursday, when Ellie came home for lunch, she saw that Mom had hung a blue-star service flag in the living room window. The flag made the house look unfamiliar, as if Pop had grown a mustache or Mom had dyed her hair blond. Ellie could barely look at it. It was yet another reminder that Jimmy was gone.

But on Friday, glorious Friday, there was a letter for Miss Eleanor McKelvey in Jimmy's slanted, sloppy boy writing. And letters for Mom and Pop and Sal, as well.

"Mom!" she screamed, tearing through the house. "Mail from Jimmy!"

"Shhh," Mom hissed, putting Ellie's lunch on the table. "Toots is asleep." Then she whispered, "Is there one for me, too? Now sit down and eat your lunch."

But Ellie was too happy for a peanut butter sandwich. She read the letter a dozen times before Mom shooed her out the door. All afternoon she patted her dress pocket, feeling the reassuring crinkle of the envelope. Whenever she peeked at the hall clock, the hands seemed stuck at two-fifteen. She couldn't wait to share her letter with Stan after school. Then Miss Granberry caught Ellie looking out at the clock and closed the door. Now time really seemed to stand still.

Finally three o'clock arrived. The girls stood in one line,

the boys in the other, splitting in the hallway to go out their separate exits. Not for the first time did Ellie think, Why do we have to go out different doors? Why do we have a boys' play yard and a girls' play yard? Does Miss Deetch think we'll catch each other's cooties?

Out in the main schoolyard, Ellie scouted around the boys' side. She spotted Stan's maroon plaid jacket by the bike racks and waved to him.

"Race you to the park," he called. "Usual place."

"No fair!" she screamed, dashing after him. "You got a head start."

"Tough toenails," Stan hollered back.

"Oh, so's your old man," Ellie shouted happily. Her saddle shoes crunched through the leaves, sending up a peppery smell that made her feel invincible. It was Friday. She had a letter from Jimmy. The world was A-OK with Ellie McKelvey.

Vaulting over a hedge, she landed at their meeting place, the fieldstone picnic shelter. Stan, in his sheepskin flyer's helmet and goggles, stood on the low wall, arms out, swaying in the wind.

"Captain Midnight has the enemy in his sights. *EEEYow!*" he said, in his best imitation of a P-38 Lightning. He aimed his index fingers and fired. "*Ack-ack-ack.* Ker-POW! Ker-POW! Ker-POW!" He dipped his "wings" in a jerky spiral. "Another Jap Zero bites the dust!"

Spying Ellie, he hopped off the wall. "What's up, doc?" he greeted her, Bugs Bunny–style.

"I've got a letter from Jimmy!"

"Swell. What's he say?" Stan shoved up his goggles. "Killed any Nazis yet?" He plunked himself on a picnic table.

"Of course not, you goof." Ellie sat next to him. "He's in boot camp." She shook out the letter and read.

Monday, October 4, 1943
Fort Jackson, South Carolina

Dear Movie Star,

Remember I said I didn't know where my next meal was coming from? I polished off Trudy's lunch before we hit Altoona. Turns out, it wasn't until we got to camp. We were so hungry we could've eaten bricks, and we just about did! The cooks were leaving for town when we pulled in, and they were not happy to see us. They slapped together the world's thickest baloney sandwiches, slicing the bread and meat any which way. I could hardly get mine in my mouth, but I managed!

I'm now a corpsman in the Army Medical Corps. That's like being an orderly at a hospital, only with a snappier uniform. The important thing is, I don't carry a gun. I'll probably spend the war emptying bed-pans and that's A-OK with me!! The guys already call me Doc—but then they call all the corpsmen Doc! It beats "Hey, you!"

Here is what I have learned so far:

1. Don't volunteer for anything. That's how you wind up with the crummy jobs, like cleaning latrines (that's Army talk for bathrooms).

2. No matter what size you are, the uniforms don't fit.

3. There are two kinds of fellows here, Lana Turner guys and the ones who like Betty Grable.

4. Anyone who says Army food is great is full of hooey. For breakfast, we have creamed chipped beef on toast. The guys call it something else, but I can't tell you what because it's dirty. They also have this runny white stuff that I thought was cream of wheat. The Southern boys call it grits. They say it's made out of corn, but you could fool me!

5. I have learned to be at the front of the chow line in the mess hall (mess is a good word for some of the food)! Lollygaggers get leftovers and that ain't good!

I have made a friend, a guy named Max Johnson. He's an orphan, so he doesn't have anybody to write him. I hear mail call is the high point of the day. Could you ask Toots to write him a letter?

It's almost time for evening chow, and you know what that means. Jimmy McKelvey to the front of the line!

Your brother, Jimmy (aka Doc)

That's it?" Stan sounded disappointed. "He hasn't met Joe DiMaggio yet?"

"That's it. I don't think DiMaggio is at Fort Jackson. He volunteered a long time before Jimmy." Ellie refolded the letter. There was a whole second page, with a postscript, but that part was not for sharing.

P.S. Have you ever noticed the North Star? They say that if you follow it, you will always find your way home. When you see it, know that wherever I am, I can see it too and am thinking about home and you. Say a little prayer for me, and I'll say one for you. Deal?

Ellie stared at the red and gold leaves at her feet. *I'll say a million prayers, God, if you keep Jimmy safe,* she promised. *And thank you for not making him a Marine. Amen.*

"Good thing your aunt moved in," Stan said, interrupting her thoughts. "Kinda takes Jimmy's place."

"She does *not* take Jimmy's place," Ellie snapped.

"I mean she keeps you from missing Jimmy too much," Stan backtracked.

"Nothing can keep me from missing Jimmy," Ellie shouted. "Especially not Toots!"

Stan threw up his hands. "Don't get all squirrelly on me again."

"I am not squirrelly!"

Stan's jackrabbit mind had already hopped on. "Doesn't

she have a war job? Do you think she makes bombs?" He scooped up a handful of acorns and fired them at a chipmunk. "Ka-pow, ka-pow, bombs over Tokyo! Stan Kozelle, flying ace, wins the war!" The chipmunk scampered away, escaping the acorn bombs.

"Beats me. It's supposed to be a secret." Ellie sighed. "And now Mom's going to work there, too."

Stan's jaw dropped. "Your mom's gonna be Rosie the Riveter?"

"Yeah. Maybe *she's* gone squirrelly." Ellie flicked acorns off the picnic table. "She starts next week. That means I can't go anywhere until an adult comes home. Or wakes up."

"You get to be in charge of yourself? You lucky duck." Stan's voice dripped envy.

"Oh yeah? *This* lucky duck gets to do all the cooking and washing and ironing."

"Doesn't Sal have to pitch in?"

"Nope. At least not as much as me. She doesn't get home from school until late afternoon."

"Yeah, but . . ." War whoops drowned out the rest. A second later, Victoria crashed through the underbrush, followed by half the sixth grade. The boy half.

"Oh, swell," muttered Ellie.

"Scram," Victoria ordered when she got within screaming distance.

"Oh yeah? Says who?" Stan demanded.

"The Marines, that's who," snarled Victoria. In her arms

she cradled the largest collection of toy guns that Ellie had seen in years. A tommy gun, BB guns, an air rifle with a missing trigger, and a holster with six-shooters slung around her hips.

The rest of the gang carried makeshift weapons of cardboard, broom handles, or just plain sticks. Jellyneck lugged a dummy drill rifle that he had found who knows where.

"Where'd you get the heavy artillery?" Stan sounded impressed.

"Yeah," Ellie chimed in. "I thought everybody gave their metal toys to the scrap drive. Hey, Victoria, weren't you in charge of that? How come you still have the guns?"

"Not that it's any of your beeswax, but they belong to my brothers. I can't give away their stuff without asking them." Victoria jutted her chin in a way that reminded Ellie of Hitler's pal Mussolini, the Italian dictator.

"But you can *play* with them without asking?" Ellie fired back.

Victoria threw down her weapons, fists clenched.

"Now you've done it," Stan whispered to Ellie.

"Are we playing war or not?" Ralph Stankavitch asked. "I gotta be home by dark."

"Keep your shirt on. Okay, you, you, and you, you, you." Victoria picked off boys with a wave of her hand. "We're the Marines. The rest of yunzes are Japs."

"How come I'm always a Jap?" Jellyneck asked.

"Because I said so!" said Victoria. "Of course, I can take my guns and go home."

"Oh, all right," Jellyneck grumbled.

"Can we play?" Stan asked, eyeing the arsenal.

"Sure. Here." Victoria tossed him a BB gun. "You're on my side."

"What about Ellie?" Stan jerked his thumb in her direction.

"Yeah," Victoria drawled. "She can play. She can be a nurse. A Jap nurse."

A Jap nurse! "No, thanks." Ellie stood and brushed off her skirt.

"Suit yourself." Victoria shrugged. "Okay, Japs, yunzes go over in the woods. Marines, this shelter is our outpost on Guadalcanal. The Japs are going to try to take it."

"But yunz got all the guns," Ralph whined.

"I could go home," Victoria reminded him.

"I *am* going home," Ellie snapped. "C'mon, Stan."

She had gone only a few steps when she realized she was walking by herself. Stan was happily firing his empty BB gun at enemy squirrels.

"Stan!" Ellie hollered. "You coming?"

"Nah," he shouted back. "See you later."

Ellie stomped off through the woods without a backward glance. Just goes to show you can't always tell who is the enemy, she thought—sometimes it's your own best friend.

7

Ellie waited for Stan to apologize. And waited. They joined the rest of the sixth grade at the Liberty matinee on Saturday, saw each other at Sunday school, and still Stan said nothing.

So, first thing Monday, Ellie ignored him. She skipped their usual before-school marbles game. With Mom starting her job, Ellie brought her lunch to school. She ate her sandwich alone, pretending to read a Nancy Drew book. Thanks to Mom's new regime, she scurried straight home at three. Stan didn't notice. He was too busy with Victoria and her sixth-grade Marines.

"What gives?" he asked, finally snaring Ellie before school Wednesday. "You haven't talked to me all week."

"If you don't know, I'm not going to tell you," she snapped.

"I *don't* know what's wrong!" Stan hollered.

"Figure it out!" Ellie shouted, and stomped off.

It was a long, lonely week. The house was so quiet that when Ellie opened the front door, she could hear Toots snoring upstairs. By Friday, Ellie couldn't remember exactly why she wanted Stan to apologize.

Saturday morning, Ellie sat cross-legged on her bed, writing a letter to Jimmy.

"Peanut," Sal yelled from downstairs, "get down here and help with the wash!"

"In a minute," Ellie yelled back.

"What?" Sal screamed. "I can't hear you."

Across the hall, a door banged open. "Hey you two, knock it off!" A pajamaed Toots stood in the hall, hands on hips, hair on end.

"Sorry," Ellie said.

"Oops," called Sal from the stairs. "I forgot you work Friday nights."

"You bet I do." Toots growled, her voice gravelly with sleep. "And I like to sleep L-A-T-E on Saturdays! Got that?" She slammed her door so hard, pictures danced on the wall.

Tiptoeing, Ellie and Sal met on the stairs to continue.

"I'm writing Jimmy," Ellie said to her red-faced and sweaty sister. Even Sal could look crummy sometimes, she thought with a touch of surprise. "Where's Mom?"

"At Corsiglia's, food shopping. She told me to finish the wash, and you're supposed to help." Sal swiped at her damp forehead.

"I'll only be a minute with the letter," Ellie pleaded.

"See that you are," Sal said in her bossiest big-sister voice. "I want to go to the matinee. If we don't get the wash done, I won't be able to go."

Ellie had forgotten about the movies. "Can I go with you?" she asked quickly.

"Why? Aren't you going with that motley bunch you run around with?"

"Oh, *them*," Ellie flipped a careless hand. "They're so immature. I don't go around with them anymore. So can I go with you?"

"Heck, no. And if you aren't in the basement in five minutes, I'll drag you down by your braids."

"All right, all right."

Back in her room, Ellie flopped on her bed to reread the letter one last time.

Saturday, October 16, 1943

Dear Jimmy,

How are you? Have you operated on anybody yet? Maybe you will save somebody's life.

Things are all screwy here with Mom working. The wash doesn't get done on Friday and we do it on Saturday. Me and Sal take turns making supper. Mom gets home too late, and Toots is a terrible cook. She's so bad she burns water! Sal isn't so good either. She's always trying out terrible things from home ec class, like tomato Jell-O (she calls it aspic) and prune whip. I make salmon pea wiggle because it's easy, but you already know that's pretty terrible, too.

Pop gets home later and later these days. A couple more of the postmen at his post office got drafted, so they're doubling up on mail routes.

We take baths at night now, because Toots hogs the bathroom when she gets home from work. She can't get over our indoor plumbing. You never saw anybody so excited over flushing the you-know-what!

I miss you and look for our star every morning and evening, first and last thing.

Love, Ellie   xoxoxo

P.S. I am making you a surprise for Christmas. You're still coming home, aren't you?

She folded the letter into the addressed envelope, and hurried downstairs to put it in the mailbox. She walked out the front door . . . and smack into Stan.

"Are you a mind reader?" he asked. "I didn't even ring the doorbell."

"So what are you doing here?" Ellie didn't mean for it to sound as nasty as it did.

"What's eating you?" Stan raised his eyebrows. "I came to see if you wanted to go to the eleven o'clock show and stay for the matinee."

A week's worth of loneliness lifted from Ellie's heart. Maybe Sal would let her off laundry duty. "Well, gee," she began. "I don't know if . . ."

"Hurry up," shouted a familiar voice. "All the good seats are gonna be gone." On the sidewalk, Victoria jogged in place, waving her arms to stay warm. Behind her, the rest of the crew entertained themselves by shoving each other off the curb and pitching rocks at the trolley rails.

"C'mon," Stan urged Ellie. "Victoria doesn't like to wait."

Ellie felt the blood rise in her neck. "Isn't that too bad."

"What yunz doin' up there?" someone hollered. "Smoochin'?"

That did it!

"Even if I could, I wouldn't go to the show with you in a million years," Ellie snapped. "I hope you and Victoria are very happy together." She slammed the door so hard, the doorbell jingled.

Upstairs, a door crashed open. "All right!" shouted Toots. "Who slammed that door?"

"Ellie, get your heinie down here," Sal screamed from the basement.

"Sorry, Toots. Coming, Sal." Ellie slunk off to the cellar. Life was just *so* unfair!

Right after lunch, Sal's chums arrived to take her to the movies. Ellie could hear them giggling and squealing in the living room. "What a bunch of birdbrains," she mumbled as she cleared the lunch table.

"You run along," Mom said. "I can redd up the kitchen. Get two dimes out of my pocketbook, and scoot."

Ellie put on her jacket, knotted a babushka under her chin, and trudged out the door. As the wind shoved her along the sidewalk, Ellie thought about the good old days. Sitting in the balcony with the other sixth graders, throwing peanuts and popcorn at the little kids downstairs. Scattering when the usher came up to check. Victoria Gandeck had been just another kid in her class, not her new sworn enemy. And Stan had been *her* best friend, not Victoria's. The good old days.

Last Saturday.

Kids streamed past Ellie toward the theater, eager to get out of the cold. Others crowded into Green's for a supply of movie snacks. No one in their right mind would eat the stale candy from the Liberty's vending machine. Bridget Flaherty and some of the sixth-grade girls stood in the ticket line, swinging their sacks of Green's popcorn, peanuts, and candy. Even though they had been in the same class since kindergarten, Ellie didn't know them very well. She hadn't needed to.

Inside the warm theater, Ellie breathed in the fragrance of stale popcorn, dusty stage drapes, and sweaty wool jackets.

Sal and her pals huddled in the lobby, looking bored. Ellie knew they were really looking for boys. She sidled over. Maybe they wouldn't notice if she followed them in.

No such luck.

"Get lost," Sal muttered, giving Ellie a nudge. *Hmm*. Looked to Ellie like Sal had stuffed her brassiere with socks again.

"Am-scray, kid," added a blonde with a lot of lipstick. "That's pig Latin for 'hit the road.' You're making us look bad."

"You don't need me to look bad," Ellie retorted, and sauntered away as if it didn't matter. Only it did. A lot.

Ellie found a seat in the middle of a row toward the back. After tripping over a dozen pairs of feet, she discovered a coat across it. Ellie tossed it to the third-grade boy in the next seat.

"Hey, I was saving," the boy protested.

"Tough toenails," said Ellie, squirming out of her jacket. She settled into the worn plush seat and waited for the lights to go down. Nothing could bother her here. Not arithmetic, not war, and certainly not Stanley Kozelle and Victoria Gandeck.

Plock. Something hit Ellie in the back of her head. *Plock.* She put her hand to her collar. Peanuts. *Plock. Plock.* More peanuts.

"Hey, Ellie," Victoria shouted over the hubbub. "Bombs over Tokyo, Ellie. Nice seat there with the third graders. Is that your boyfriend?"

Ellie slumped to avoid the peanut bombs.

Plock. Plock. Plock.

Two cartoons, a Three Stooges short, a newsreel, a reminder to buy war bonds, and a main feature later, Ellie emerged from the theater, squinting in the sun. She picked a peanut shell from a braid as Victoria charged past her.

"Everybody meet at Green's," she shouted. "They've got new comic books."

Ellie set off in the opposite direction, toward Millionaire's Row. She knew real millionaires like the Mellons and Heinzes didn't live there; they lived across the river, in Shadyside. But the houses on the Row were the biggest in Ellie's neighborhood. These homes belonged to older people, with adult children—if anyone from there had ever gone to her school, they had graduated long ago. The only Row resident Ellie knew personally was Dr. Atkinson, whose office was in his house. Yep, there it was, a pink Spanish-looking house with a tile roof, and a Lincoln Zephyr in the driveway.

Ellie enjoyed looking at the big houses. Two-story fieldstones with porches and turrets and balconies. Manicured yards, not a stray leaf in sight. Big, shiny Packards and Lincolns in the driveways, ration stickers plastered to the windshields. "C" stickers, the best kind. No gas rationing for doctors and judges and other "essential war workers," as the Rationing Board called them.

Windows glowed with lamplight as the sun dipped behind the treetops. Ellie watched the scenes inside, like a different movie at every house. In a red brick, a maid poured from a silver teapot as two elderly women held up china cups. A little girl with Shirley Temple curls pounded out a jerky little tune at a grand piano. Ellie decided she was a visiting granddaughter.

Big cement lions guarded her favorite house. Ellie

paused on the sidewalk to admire them. Then, discovering a hole in the boxwood hedge, she wedged herself in so she could get a closer look inside.

Through the diamond-shaped windowpanes, she studied a man and woman in evening clothes, sitting in deep leather chairs. Maybe they were going someplace fancy, like the opera. The man wrote on a folded newspaper. A crossword puzzle? The woman stitched something in a needlework frame. Ellie gazed at the scene, enchanted.

Not that the people themselves were terribly interesting. To Ellie, the play of soft light from silk-shaded lamps, the unhurried movements of their hands, the elegant drape of their clothes seemed to be from another world, far away from Macken Street. She couldn't imagine having time to sit and do almost nothing. And all dressed up, to boot!

Whish-rattle-rattle. "Dad-ratted chain!" squeaked a male voice.

Ellie startled out of her trance. At the curb, a Western Union boy tinkered with the chain drooping from his bike gears. He was one of Sal's high school pals, Fred Somebody. Ellie couldn't remember his last name, just that he worked on the weekend. Chain back in place, he wiped his greasy hands on a hanky and mounted the bike. Ellie shivered, shrinking further into shrubbery. Western Union telegrams were almost always bad news. Holding her breath and crossing her fingers, she willed Fred away from the house.

But Fred steered up the circular drive of the lions' house. He nudged the kickstand with his heel, then marched up the stone walk, his footsteps like whip cracks in the frosty air. For the first time, Ellie saw the service flag on the front door. Silk, with gold fringe and a single blue star.

Fred tugged at his jacket, squared his shoulders, and rang the doorbell. Ellie froze, not wanting to see, unable to go.

The massive door swung open, flag fluttering. Light spilled across the stone steps as a uniformed maid talked to Fred. He took off his cap and held up the telegram. The maid closed the door.

Fred must have come to the wrong house, Ellie thought with relief. But when she turned back to the window, she saw the maid enter the softly lit room and speak to the man and woman. For a long moment, they did not move. Pencil stilled in midair. Needle glinting in the soft light, hand trembling.

Slowly, the man rose and helped the woman to her feet. Ellie wasn't sure they were even moving until they disappeared from view. The front door swung open, and there they stood, clutching each other, heads bowed.

Ellie scrambled out of the bushes and started running. She was halfway down the block when she heard the scream. No, not a scream—a howl.

She ran past the Packards and balconies and spotless yards. Back up Macken Street. Past the Liberty. Past Corsiglia's market. Past St. Matthew's, and down the street to Green's.

Because there were worse things than sitting alone at the movies with peanut shells in your hair. Enemies worse than Victoria Gandeck. And sometimes you have to forgive people, even when you think they're wrong. Ellie hoped Stan was still at Green's.

She needed her best friend.

8

The bright blue days of October had given way to the battleship gray of November. With winter on the way, Ellie was happy that she was no longer going home at lunch to check the mail.

Sleet peppered the windows of Room Seven. The daily sandwich swap in Miss Granberry's room was under way. Not that Ellie was swapping her peanut butter sandwich; she loved peanut butter. A good thing, since nowadays she made her own lunch.

"Anybody wanna trade?" Stan held up a sandwich, neatly wrapped in wax paper.

"Whatcha got?" asked Bridget, peering into her lunch sack.

Stan opened an end of the wax paper. "Cream cheese with olives. How 'bout you?"

"Tongue." Bridget wrinkled her nose. Tongue wasn't rationed, so there was plenty to go around, which was about all you could say for it.

"Yuck," Victoria said. Ellie didn't think much of Victoria's lunch either, salami on rye. Very smelly salami, at that.

"With horseradish?" Stan asked Bridget. She nodded. "Hand it over." He tossed Bridget the wax paper packet, as she passed him her unwrapped slabs of rye, scraps of tongue dangling from the edges. Every day, Stan traded a perfectly good sandwich for something disgusting, like a string bean sandwich or tongue, and never ate his second one from home.

Jellyneck skittered into the room, rain dripping from his hedgehog hair.

"Gosh, why'd you go home?" Bridget asked, daintily nibbling her new sandwich. "It's sleeting cats and dogs."

Jellyneck's sneakers squished as he headed for the cloakroom, ignoring the question.

"Oscar." Miss Granberry looked up from her desk. "Drape your jacket across the radiator to dry." Why had Ellie never noticed Jellyneck's threadbare jacket elbows, the neatly mended rip in back? How many brothers had worn that jacket before him?

Jellyneck dropped into the seat behind Stan. Stan turned around. "I'm full to the tonsils, and I have another sandwich here. You want it?" Jellyneck nodded, and wolfed it down as if he hadn't eaten in a week.

"Anybody got a letter?" Stan asked, looking at Ellie.

"Jimmy dropped me a line," she said, trying to look casual.

"Swell," said Stan, as if he hadn't already seen it. "You gonna read it to us?"

Ellie cleared her throat.

Dear Movie Star,

The Army is keeping me busy. So far, most of the things I have learned have to do with blood. How to take blood pressure, draw blood, tie a tourniquet, stuff like that. I'm turning into a regular vampire!

It's still warm here, which isn't so good for those twenty-mile marches we take. I'm homesick for snow!

It's almost taps. That's Army for lights-out. Just when you think you're too old for someone to tell you it's bedtime, along comes the Army!

Your brother, Doc Jimmy

"Swell stuff," said Stan, folding his lunch bag to use again.

"Big deal," sniffed Victoria. She pulled a letter from her pocket and read:

Dear Little Sis,

Can't say where I am, but it's an island and it's hot and we're looking for snipers. Them Japs are sneaky, hiding in trees. We watch for smoke. That means a sniper is smoking a cig. Then you watch the tree trunk for

Victoria dropped her voice to a loud whisper.

P-I-S-S. They do that in the trees so we won't see them, they think. I nailed a couple that way already.

The islanders are so happy to see GIs, they give us gifts all the time. I got enough native knives and daggers to arm the whole sixth grade! I'm still going to get you that Jap flag I promised. And one of them whatchamacallit swords. A sayonara sword? That don't look right, but I can hardly spell English, let alone Jap. Ha ha!

Remember me to Macken Street and keep your nose clean, kid. I'll be home before you know it.

Your big brother, Buddy

"Zowie." Jellyneck licked cream cheese from his lip. "A real Jap sword."

Stan snatched the letter from Victoria. "I want to read about the snipers again."

"Did he really say 'piss'?" asked Ralph.

"Hey, yunz are getting it all smeary." Victoria grabbed the letter back.

Ellie slumped in her desk. Even Victoria's letters are better than mine, she fumed.

Miss Granberry clapped her hands for attention. "Students, lunch hour is over. Now let's prepare ourselves for the afternoon. Dispose of your lunch wrappers, and get out your arithmetic books."

Ellie stumped up to the wastebasket with her wax paper, her mood decidedly sour. Her bad mood lasted until the middle of arithmetic when she heard . . .

"It's snowing!" The whisper rippled up and down the rows. Sure enough, the sleet had turned to snow. It always snowed before Thanksgiving.

The first holiday without Jimmy.

Victoria threw open a window and leaned out. Cold whooshed through the room, swirling papers off desks. "The snow is sticking to the sled hill," she announced.

The whispers rose to a buzz. The first sledding of the year was always the best.

"Victoria Gandeck, close that window immediately." Miss Granberry thumped her ruler for attention. "One would think you had never seen snow before."

Ellie stared at the fat, wet flakes piling up on the stone window ledge.

"Eleanor, stop woolgathering and come to the chalkboard, please." Snapping to attention, Ellie started for the front of the room.

"Your arithmetic homework, Eleanor?" Miss Granberry reminded her. "Could you work example 12 for the class, please?"

Ellie couldn't believe that Miss Granberry had picked the one problem she didn't do! She grabbed the undone homework from her desk and slouched to the blackboard. On her way, she glanced out the door at the big hall clock. Two forty-five. Fifteen minutes until school was out.

Phooey.

Picking up the chalk, Ellie wrote *233 × 499*, and drew a line under it. The line was a little crooked, so she erased it and drew a straighter one. Sweat trickled down her backbone. The radiators hissed and knocked. The room smelled of pencil shavings and Vitalis and Victoria's salami sandwich wrappings in the trash.

Thwack. Thwack. Thwack. Miss Granberry whacked the ruler in her palm. The sound drove any arithmetic thoughts right out of Ellie's head. Even though she knew it was wrong, she quickly scratched *1,227* as the answer, and scuttled back to her seat.

"Now, class." Toward the end of the day, Miss Granberry's voice squeaked like chalk. "Who can correct Eleanor's mistake?"

Victoria's hand shot straight up in the air, like a *Heil Hitler.* Briskly, she marched to the board, snatched the eraser, smeared away Ellie's feeble efforts, and rapidly chalked in the correct answer.

"Very good," said Miss Granberry. Victoria swished back to her seat with a pleased smile.

Show-off, Ellie seethed. Know-it-all.

At long last, the class went to the cloakroom for their wraps and lined up at the door.

"Eleanor," Miss Granberry croaked, her voice barely audible. "Please remain."

Ellie trudged back to her desk, dropping into her seat like a sack of potatoes. She couldn't imagine what Miss Granberry wanted. She stared at her desktop, where some long-ago student had carved *Sean O'Toole* into the worn oak. Wherever Sean O'Toole was now, he was better off than Ellie McKelvey, missing the first snow.

Creak creak creak sang the floorboards as Miss Granberry came ever-so-slowly down the aisle. Hurry up, Ellie thought, tracing Sean O'Toole's name with her finger.

"Eleanor, did I hear you reading a letter from your brother during lunch? Is he still in basic training?"

"Yes, ma'am. He's in South Carolina," said Ellie. "But he'll be home for Christmas."

"Will he, now?" Miss Granberry's silver eyebrows came together in a puzzled line.

"Yes, ma'am, but the war will be over by then, won't it?"

The teacher started to say something, then patted Ellie's shoulder instead. "I hope so, dear. Now run along."

Ellie was at the door before Miss Granberry called, "Eleanor, Mr. Hitler will not be around forever, but I assure you that multiplication will. Please redo today's homework."

"Yes, ma'am. Good night, Miss Granberry."

Outside, Ellie gulped the deliciously icy air. The frosty lungful made her feel frisky, like a squirrel. She'd have to tell Stan, "Hey, I really am squirrelly!"

She wasn't the only one who felt squirrelly. Snow turned the kids into shrieking animals. Sliding on the slick walks. Throwing snowballs. In a corner of the play yard, a couple of optimistic first graders struggled to roll the bottom boulder of a snowman. Ralph had Stan in a headlock, scrubbing his face with snow.

"Scram, Sam," he told Stan when he saw Ellie.

"What did Granberry want?" Stan asked, brushing the snow off his jacket. "Careful, it's slippy."

Ellie picked her way across the playground, wishing she had worn her galoshes. "I have to do that arithmetic homework over. And she asked about Jimmy. Wonder why?"

"Who knows?" Stan stuck out his tongue, caught a snowflake, then grinned. "Let's go sledding."

"I have to let Aunt Toots know where I'm going. I hope she's awake." She blinked to keep snow from sticking to her lashes.

"Don't forget your sled," added Stan, as they stamped up Ellie's porch steps.

Ellie jiggled the doorknob. Locked. "Aunt Toots, I'm home," she shouted, banging on the door. "Maybe she's washing her hair or something."

"With the door locked?" Stan said. "Who locks their door when they're home?"

Opening the door with her latchkey, Ellie stepped into the entry with Stan.

"There's a note," Stan said, pointing to a sheet of tablet paper on the lamp table.

Kiddos,

Heard a butcher in West View has some beef. Don't know when I'll be back. Put potatoes and carrots on to boil.

Toots

"I guess you aren't coming, are you?" Stan headed for the door, rezipping his jacket.

"I guess not," said Ellie, sighing as she took off her coat. "She could be in line forever."

Stan lingered in the entry, flapping his wet mittens.

"So go sled," said Ellie, not caring how cross she sounded.

"Uh, can I borrow your sled?"

"Use your own sled."

"Can't. I gave it to the Commandos' scrap drive. The iron runners, you know."

"Oh, all right! Wait here." She stomped to the cellar.

"Ick." She shook stringy cobwebs from her hands as she reached behind the furnace for her sled. With everyone turning their Flexible Flyers into scrap, Ellie's wooden-runner hand-me-down was one of the few left.

"Here," she said, shoving the sled at Stan and locking the door behind him. "Have fun," she yelled.

The house was quiet, save for the furnace wheezing through the floor vents. Too quiet. Ellie slipped on Mom's coverall apron and clicked on the kitchen radio. "Boogie Woogie Bugle Boy" blasted into the room. Getting out the vegetable peeler, she whacked at the carrots in time to the music. But even the Andrews Sisters didn't cheer her up.

The snow fell thicker and faster. Across the alley, she could barely see the Gandecks' garage. She hoped that at least her sled was having a good time.

"And now, news from the war front," a voice boomed from the radio.

"Oh no you don't." Ellie snapped it off. The only news she wanted to hear was that the war was over.

Putting the vegetables on to boil, she went upstairs. She decided to change clothes, knit Jimmy's Christmas scarf, and maybe do some homework. But Jimmy's closed door was like a blow to the head. Jimmy had never closed his door.

Without thinking, she put her hand on the doorknob to Toots's . . . no—*Jimmy's*—room. Just this once. She wanted to see his things. Pretend he was home.

Ellie pushed open the door.

The iron bedstead and chenille spread, the maple dresser and battered desk were still there. White walls, patched window shades, and the leaky spot on the ceiling that looked like the Liberty Bell. All the same.

But where were the model airplanes? Jimmy's baseball glove, his Pirates pennant? Ellie knew he had taken his Lana picture with him, but where was the clay ashtray she made for him in first grade? He kept it on his dresser to hold pocket change. Toots better not have thrown it out!

A wilderness of boxes and bottles had replaced Lana and the ashtray on the dresser. Evening in Paris perfume. Tussy deodorant. Wave-set. Bobby pins scattered here and there. Hair crimpers with cruel-looking teeth.

The room even smelled different. Jimmy's room had smelled like Vitalis and dirty socks. Now it reeked of Evening in Paris and the smoky-factory smell of Toots's overalls flung across the bed.

Ellie jerked open a dresser drawer, looking for the ashtray. There, in a tangle of undies and bobby socks, was a letter addressed to Miss Agnes Guilfoyle. Agnes? Oh, right. Toots's real name. From a Private Max Johnson, Fort Jackson, South Carolina. Jimmy's friend. The envelope was neatly slit down the side.

Something hard and ugly rose in Ellie's chest.

She wanted to read this letter from Max Johnson.

Only a real creep would read another person's mail. But Toots deserves it! Ellie thought. She's acting like she belongs here!

Ellie's hand shook as she pried open the tissue-thin envelope and . . .

Keys jingled in a lock, and the front door banged open.

"Helloooo," Aunt Toots caroled from downstairs.

Ellie dropped the envelope back in the drawer, as if she'd been scorched.

"Anybody home? Ellie? Sal?"

Ellie quickly shut the dresser drawer and scurried from the room, silently closing the door behind her. She met Aunt Toots on the stair landing.

"The vegetables are boiling," Ellie said in a guilty rush.

"Swell!" Toots boomed, hefting a butcher's parcel. "Beef stew tonight! It ain't filet mignon, but it ain't horsemeat, neither. These days . . ."

". . . folks take what they can get," Ellie and Aunt Toots finished together. "Owe you a nickel," they both said, laughing.

Ellie's heart warmed for a minute, as her aunt disappeared downstairs. Maybe Jimmy was right about Toots—she was a good egg after all.

Ellie could hear Toots singing "Pistol Packin' Mama," slamming cupboard doors and rattling pots and pans. "I tell you, kiddo," she said as Ellie came to the kitchen door, "I thought I'd be lonesome here, but you know what? I ain't homesick a bit."

Ellie remembered what Jimmy had written in his letter about missing snow. She knew that he was homesick, and the warmth in Ellie's heart vanished as fast as it had kindled.

"Yes, ma'am, I am fittin' in just fine!" said Toots, chopping up the stew beef.

So Toots thought she was fitting in fine, did she? Ellie watched the knife flash through the meat and she knew one thing for dead sure. The next time she was in the house alone, she would read that letter from Private Max Johnson.

9

At supper one night, a week before Thanksgiving, Ellie's mother dropped the bombshell.

"What do you mean we aren't having Thanksgiving this year?" Ellie stared at her mother. "Are you kidding?"

"Ellie, please don't talk with your mouth full. More turnips, anyone?" Mom passed the bowl to Pop as if she had said something ordinary, like "Today is Tuesday."

"The plants are staying open on Thanksgiving." Pop said, scraping the last of the mashed turnips onto his plate. "A holiday meal is just too much to ask of your mother, now that she's working."

"Not only that," Mom added, "but I checked on the price of turkey at Hales' the other day. Do you know they want fifty-nine cents a pound for a turkey? We can't afford to pay that kind of money for a Thanksgiving turkey, then turn around and do it again in a couple of weeks for Christmas as well."

Ellie played with her mashed turnips, hiding them under the stringy stewed chicken she also wasn't going to eat. "We can help, me and Sal can." But even as she said it, she knew Pop was right.

"Huh!" snorted Sal. "You know how to cook a turkey? Or are you planning to serve salmon pea wiggle?"

"No, tomato aspic," Ellie shot back.

"Girls! Enough!" said Pop, thumping his knife handle on the table.

"We'll do better for Christmas," Mom promised. "We'll save up our rations and have a feast. The plant is paying overtime to work Christmas, but Toots and I have already decided to take the day off. I'll have time to cook. It will be like old times."

And Jimmy will be home.

What's so great about Thanksgiving? Ellie said to herself over and over. When she saw the handprint turkeys in the kindergarten room windows. When they sang "Come, Ye Thankful People, Come" in assembly. After all, it was just a big dinner where everybody ate too much and the grownups told boring stories about the Good Old Days. Besides, who wanted to celebrate without Jimmy?

Ellie sat at her school desk the day before the holiday, struggling with her arithmetic homework. Homework! On Thanksgiving!

"You may have this last hour to do your homework or read," Miss Granberry had said with a rare, tiny smile. Easy enough for her to smile, Ellie thought as she erased problem four for the fifth time. Miss Granberry has the answers in the back of her book!

Laughter floated up the hall. All around Room Seven, other classes were having parties. Miss Granberry crossed the room and closed the door.

Ellie's pencil lead snapped. Good! An excuse to get up.

As she ground the sharpener handle round and round, Ellie studied the photographs on the bulletin board. Pictures of men and women, all in uniform. Some were Miss Granberry's former students. Some were relatives of sixth graders. A sort of Honor Wall of service men and women. It was the first time Ellie had looked at them. *Really* looked at them.

Closest to her, all four Gandeck boys grinned in a color snapshot taken on their front porch, caps cocked, arms slung across each other's shoulders. Ellie could almost hear them saying "Lemme at that lousy Hitler. I'll punch his lights out! Tojo and Mussolini, too!"

Next to the Gandecks, a photo-booth picture. The face under the Army cap looked familiar. She leaned in for a better look. Big ears, funny round chin, firm mouth. Of course! That was Jellyneck's oldest brother, Orrie, who had been their paperboy.

"If there's one good thing about the war," Pop said, "it's that my paper finally lands on the porch. Hope that Jelinek kid aims better with a rifle than he did with my *Post-Gazette*."

All kinds of pictures covered the wall. Newspaper clippings, black-and-white snapshots, even a few formal portraits in uniform, with the color tinted in. Sailors, soldiers, and nurses. WAVES and WACs and SPARs. Army and Navy and Marines. Army Air Force. Even some Coast Guard and Merchant Marine uniforms. Some of the faces smiled, their eyes holding a secret joke. "Can you believe I'm in a *war*?" they seemed to say. Other faces were solemn, eyes serious, as if seeing a terrible future. Their eyes said "Can you believe I'm in a war?" too, but not in a joking way.

Some pictures had tiny gold stars in the lower right hand corners. Down near the chalk rail, Bill Schmidt with a gold star. Ellie squinted at Miss Granberry's old-fashioned, spidery script, inked across the margin. *Bill Schmidt. Lost at sea, USS* Juneau, *November 1942.*

Above Bill, a stocky boy in an Army uniform with a wide smile, two beagles at his feet. *Sy Hart. Missing, presumed dead, Winter 1943. Somewhere in the Pacific.* Gold star.

Next to Sy, another sailor leaned against a car, foot on the running board, holding a girl in a tight sweater close to his side. *Otis Bennett. Lost at sea, Battle of Savo Island, August 1942.* Gold star.

Beneath him, *Sean O'Toole. Missing, somewhere over France. Presumed dead. Spring 1942.* Sean O'Toole, who had sat in her desk . . . how many years ago? As Ellie stared at the picture, the dashing young man with the Clark Gable mustache and leather flying jacket dissolved. In his place, a kid. A kid with freckles and a snaggly toothed smile, in a jersey and corduroys. He probably had marbles in his pocket, like Stan. Maybe a peashooter, too.

"Eleanor, your pencil is sufficiently sharpened." Miss Granberry's voice crackled in her ear. "Take your seat, please."

"Yes, ma'am," said Ellie. The classroom floor seemed to slant upward and her head buzzed. Somewhere between the pencil sharpener and her desk, the war became real for Ellie. The names she heard on the radio each night— Midway, Savo Island, Guadalcanal—were now real places. Places where Bill, Sy, Otis, and Sean had disappeared or died.

Ellie hadn't brought in a picture of Jimmy. He hadn't sent her one of him in uniform. Maybe the war would be over before he did.

Until then, he was safe in South Carolina, and not in a Pacific jungle like Buddy Gandeck or on a ship in the North Atlantic or a plane "somewhere over France."

As she wobbled back to her seat, Ellie knew how you could have Thanksgiving without turkey and pie.

It was as simple as knowing your brother was safe.

And that the star on your family's service flag was blue.

Not gold.

10

Ellie couldn't wait for school to start after the Thanksgiving-That-Wasn't. The calendar said November, but it couldn't fool Ellie. The Monday after Thanksgiving meant the beginning of the Christmas season.

The Macken Street storekeepers wrote "Merry Christmas" and "Season's Greetings" on their windows with white shoe polish. Maybe to disguise the bare displays, Ellie decided. Sugar and gas weren't the only things being rationed. So were rubber and metal of all kinds—and most toys were made of rubber or metal. I'm really too old for toys, Ellie reminded herself.

The Christmas season also meant that Mr. Corsiglia hung a loudspeaker outside the grocery so he could share his collection of Bing Crosby Christmas songs with the neighborhood. Whether they wanted to share them or not.

"If I hear Bing Crosby sing 'I'll Be Home for Christmas' one more time, I'll go wacky," said Ellie. She and Stan leaned against the wide windowsills of Room Seven, watching new snow fall on the old snow, which had fallen on the slushy first snow.

"What's the matter?" Stan unwrapped his egg-salad sandwich. "You don't like Bing? Bub-bub-ba-boo," he sang, imitating Bing Crosby's familiar song phrase.

Ellie didn't know how to explain that the song held both promise and disappointment for her holiday. So she didn't try.

"Nah, it's not Bing," Ellie said, looking at her own sandwich with distaste. "It's my lunch. Soy loaf. Sal made meat loaf without any meat, and a load of that soy extender junk."

"Soy loaf? You always have peanut butter."

"Sal did the marketing." Ellie took a bite, chewed, and swallowed. "And she forgot to buy peanut butter."

"Fire it my way," said Stan. "Gotta get big and strong to fight the Germans."

Ellie started to say, "Like there'll still be a war when you're eighteen." But what if there *was* still a war when Stan was eighteen? Or, worse, what if the war was over and the United States lost?

"Bub-bub-ba-boo," Stan crooned in Ellie's ear. "Gimme your sandwich, bub-bub-ba-boo."

Ellie smiled at his Bing imitation and passed him the sandwich.

Victoria swished up to the window, oozing importance from every pore. "Guess what?" she said.

"School is closed for the duration?" Stan guessed.

"I'm serious!" Victoria socked Stan's arm. "Come on, guess."

"Eleanor Roosevelt is coming to assembly tomorrow?" said Ellie.

Victoria missed the sarcasm. "She is?"

"What do you think?" Ellie shrugged. Victoria didn't blink. "Oh, all right. What's the big surprise?" Ellie's hand itched to smack her.

"My brother Frankie isn't coming home for Christmas," Victoria announced.

"Big deal," snorted Stan, and took Ellie's sandwich back to his seat.

"It is *too* a big deal," said Victoria. "It means that he's going overseas real soon."

"Really? How do you know?" A tiny tongue of fear flickered inside Ellie.

"Because he went right from boot camp to California, instead of coming home on leave like my other brothers. Frankie says they've cancelled all the home leaves, so I'll just bet he's shipping out from there."

Ellie's stomach did the Dips-swoop.

"Well, *my* brother is coming home for Christmas," said Ellie. "He said so, and he is!" At least, that's what Ellie *thought* Jimmy had told her. She waited for Victoria to say something. She didn't.

Victoria stared out into the schoolyard. "I wish things were the way they used to be," she whispered.

I know what you mean, Ellie wanted to say.

But before she could, Victoria began a loud, off-key rendition of "I'll Be Home for Christmas."

Ellie wanted to smack her all over again.

Chocolate! Ellie smelled it the minute she opened the front door after school that day. The aroma drew her into the kitchen, where racks of fresh-baked cookies covered the countertops.

"Smelled my world-famous cookies, didja?" Aunt Toots pulled a cookie sheet from the oven. In her work overalls and apron, she looked like a cross between Rosie the Riveter and Betty Crocker. But there was something else about her outfit that bugged Ellie. What is it? she wondered.

"Hey, snap out of your dream world, kiddo," said Toots. "Help me finish these cookies so I can send this box to the post office when your pop goes to work in the morning."

"What box?"

Toots spooned more brown lumps onto a cookie sheet. The lumps looked like what badly behaved dogs left on the sidewalk.

"Jimmy's Christmas box. It has to be in the mail by December 1, for somebody stateside." Toots squinted at a magazine recipe. "These don't look like the ones in this picture."

Ellie's heart gave a hard thump. She didn't know they were sending Jimmy a Christmas box.

"Have you finished knitting that scarf?" Toots asked, still studying the recipe. "We can send it with the rest of the stuff."

"Why? He'll be home for Christmas."

Toots looked up. "That's news to me, Shorty."

"He said . . . he said . . ." Ellie thought hard. "Something about keeping the Christmas tree up."

Toots rapidly loaded the contents of the cooling rack into a shoebox lined with wax paper. "Who knows? Christmas is a time of miracles, they say." She handed one of the baked lumps to Ellie. "Try this."

Ellie chewed and swallowed. "Kind of dry. Do you have any chocolate chips left?"

"I'm saving the rest of the chocolate and sugar for us," said Toots. "I've got an idea for Christmas I'll tell you about later." She pulled the pinafore apron off over her head, and suddenly Ellie knew what had been bugging her.

"Say, isn't that Jimmy's shirt?" she asked.

Toots examined the long sleeves of her green shirt, pretending great surprise. "Why, I'll be doggoned if it ain't."

Ellie frowned, but before she could speak, Toots hastily added, "Jimmy told me I could borrow anything in his closet I needed. He figures he'll gain some weight in the Army and those shirts and such won't fit him when he comes back. Now, I've got to finish packing his box. Why don't you run along and get that scarf for me, Shorty."

"It's not finished," Ellie lied, and went upstairs to change clothes. She wanted to watch Jimmy open it himself Christmas morning.

Toots must have turned on the radio because "I'll Be Home for Christmas" wafted up the stairs.

Jimmy better come home for Christmas, Ellie thought. Before Toots wears out all his shirts.

"This house is like Union Station." Pop rattled his Sunday *Post-Gazette* in disgust. "People coming and going at all hours. Whatever happened to peace and quiet?"

"If you didn't work all those double shifts, you'd know that peace around here is a thing of the past," Mom said as she brought the teapot in from the kitchen.

"Peace?" cracked Sal as she finished setting the lunch table. "Don't you know there's a war on, Pop?"

"So I've heard," said Pop, heaving himself out of his Morris chair. "Peace of any kind is mighty hard to find these days. Church is about the only peaceful place I can think of. If them Nazis and Japs spent more time on their knees, world wouldn't be in the mess it's in."

"Oh, they're all heathens," said Sal with a flip of her hair.

"Who's a heathen?" yawned Toots, staggering downstairs. "You mean me, for sleeping in? Skipping that gasbag Schuyler ever' now and then don't make me a heathen." Ellie bit back a smile. Sometimes she couldn't help liking Aunt Toots.

"Still, it seems that Sunday is the only time we're all to-gether these days," said Mom. "Time for us to catch up on what all has been going on with one another." She plunked a platter of waffles on the table. "Pull up a chair, everybody. Lunch is getting cold."

"Not lunch, Mom," Sal said in an exasperated sort of way. "It's brunch. That's what they call it at Connie Cavendish's house."

"Lunch, brunch, whatever you call it, somebody pour me some tea," said Aunt Toots. "I'd do it myself if I were awake. I need an eye-opener for sure."

The steaming tea did seem to perk Toots up a bit. After everyone had a round of waffles, Toots clinked her cup down in the saucer and cleared her throat. "I'd like to ask a favor."

"A loan till payday?" Pop grinned.

"Nothing like that." Toots folded her hands on the table in a very un-Toots-like way. "I have an idea. I wondered, since the folks aren't coming up for the holidays—"

"What?" Ellie blurted.

"Hunh?" said Sal.

"You two don't speak English?" joked Pop.

"Gramma and Grampa aren't coming for Christmas?" shrieked Ellie.

"Eleanor, ladylike voice, please," said Mom. "And no. They aren't coming this year."

"How come?" asked Sal.

"You know why," said Mom. "The President has asked

everyone not to travel unnecessarily. There's a shortage of passenger trains, with the government using so many as troop trains. The passenger trains are sidetracked to let the troop trains through. Even if they decided to come, it could take the relatives two days to get here from West Virginia."

"How come we didn't know about this before?" Ellie demanded.

"Like I said." Mom sighed and poured herself another cup of tea. "Seems like we just don't see much of each other these days."

Ellie couldn't imagine Christmas without Gramma's chocolate pies and sacks of pecans from the farm. Or the smell of Grampa's pipe that lingered long after he'd gone.

"Can't they drive?" But Ellie knew the answer. Gasoline was rationed and so were tires. The McKelveys' Ford had been up on blocks in the garage since Pearl Harbor.

"The sorry fact," said Pop, "is that unless something unusual happens, the relatives won't be here for the duration."

Ellie dug her nails into her palms. There it was again—those three awful words.

Aunt Toots cleared her throat. "Well, as I was saying, some of the gang at work can't get home for Christmas either, and I can't imagine anything worse than spending Christmas in a boardinghouse . . ."

I can, thought Ellie. Christmas without Gramma and Grampa, and *with* Toots.

"You want to invite these friends of yours over for Christmas, is that it?" Pop asked.

"Not for dinner, but maybe just for the evening or . . ." Toots sounded almost shy.

"Nonsense," Mom interrupted. "Who knows if their boardinghouse will even serve a meal that day. We'll make the food stretch."

That was Toots's big idea? A bunch of strangers for Christmas, and they would have to make the food stretch? Ellie knew she was being selfish, but she didn't care. She didn't want to spend Christmas with people she didn't know, and make the food stretch. She had a sudden horrible vision of Sal's soy loaf, the all-time champion of food-stretching meals, being served along with turkey and cranberries.

"Are any of your friends boys?" Sal asked, trying to sound casual. Ellie knew better.

"Just one, a 4-F'er named Wally," said Toots.

"Oh," Sal said. "What's wrong with him? Does he have two heads or something?"

"He's got a bum leg," said Toots. "Although it isn't none of my business. Yours either." Seeing Sal's face fall, she added, "What did you expect? That's why he's 4-F. All the able-bodied fellas are in the service."

"Connie Cavendish only dates men in uniform," said Sal.

"I'm so happy for Connie Cavendish," commented Mom dryly. "It's all settled. Toots's friends will be here for Christmas. Girls, if you're finished, you may clear the table."

"Yes, Mom," said Ellie, stacking the sticky plates. Things weren't settled at all. *At least Jimmy will be home.*

But what if he wasn't?

Ellie turned on the kitchen taps full blast, drowning out the thought.

11

Ellie jiggled the front doorknob. Locked. Good. Toots had gone somewhere, and she, Ellie, would be alone. All alone in the house.

Letting herself in, she shouted, "Anybody home?" just to make sure.

Only the furnace wheezing through the floor vent answered. A note was propped on the lamp table.

Kiddos,

Santa and me are out shopping. Won't be home until dinnertime. There's chicken livers in the icebox for supper.

Toots

Ellie's stomach squeezed with excitement. There would be time to read that letter from Max Whoosis. And to look for her ashtray.

But first, supper.

Opening the refrigerator, Ellie located the dripping meat package. Her tongue curled with distaste. Liver hash, she decided. At least the onions and potatoes would help. She set to work, peeling potatoes, chopping onions, then setting it all back in the refrigerator.

Ellie ran upstairs, considered doing homework or knitting on the Christmas presents she was making for the family, instead of snooping. Then she marched across the hall and gave Toots's doorknob a yank.

The bed was covered with letters, lots of them. Some opened, some not, some half-finished replies, strewn across the chenille bedspread. Ellie riffled through a stack of sealed envelopes. Letters to girls in Lost Gap. To soldiers Ellie had never heard of. To Gramma and Grampa.

Best of all, resting on the pillow like a crown jewel was a letter from Max. An *opened* letter from Max. Hot dog! Gingerly, Ellie picked up the letter, all thoughts of searching for the ashtray forgotten.

Dear Miss Agnes,

Miss Agnes? Obviously, Max was no sweet-talker.

Boring, too. Ellie scanned the page. Bad food, long marches, horsing around with the fellows. She had read it all before, and funnier, in Jimmy's letters. But at the bottom of the page was an arrow pointing to the back. Ellie flipped the page.

P.S. Looks like Jim and I are going to have a Christmas surprise. The Army says we're not to say a word, so I'll write more about that later.

A Christmas surprise? What else could it be but that the Army was giving Christmas leaves? Jimmy must be coming home and keeping it a secret. That big faker Toots would play along as if Jimmy were spending the holiday at Fort Jackson! Well, if Toots could playact, Ellie could too.

The ticking clock on the bedside table reminded Ellie that Toots would be back any minute. She scampered downstairs to finish supper.

Ellie tap-danced around the dining room, slapping down plates and silverware as she set the table. Then back to the kitchen, slamming drawers and cupboard doors, just to let off steam. *Jimmy really is coming home!*

"Aren't we the bluebird of happiness?" Sal stamped the snow from her feet on the kitchen doormat. "What gives?"

"I'm dreaming of a white Christmas," Ellie sang, dumping liver and onions into a pan.

Sal shrugged. "Big deal. It's always a white Christmas in Pittsburgh."

Over the sizzle of frying livers, Ellie heard the front door scrape open, then slam, followed by more foot-stomping in the front hall.

"Nobody come out here," Toots bellowed. "I got Santy Claus with me, and he don't want your Christmas ruint."

Stomp-stomp-stomp. Toots's boots on the stairs to her room. No one would call her light on her feet. *Tromp-tromp-tromp* back down to the kitchen.

"Them chicken livers smell good." Toots sniffed the pan. "You chop onion in them?"

"Yep." Ellie poked the livers with a long fork.

"Thought so," said Toots. "Them onions are so powerful, I swear I could smell 'em in my room. With the door closed, too."

Ellie realized she had forgotten to wash her hands before she went into Toots's room. Did Toots know? Or was she just being Toots?

Mr. Corsiglia's Christmas trees were propped outside the grocery. Ellie and Stan braved the Bing Crosby recital on the loudspeaker to inspect the crop at least once a day.

"It has to be perfect," Ellie said, studying a tall spruce. She and Jimmy had always bought the tree together, examining every one before choosing. Was the trunk straight? Needles too dry? The shape full and bushy? Then, afterward, they'd go to Green's for hot chocolate.

"It had better be perfect," Stan commented, "it's a whole dollar. Your folks are gonna pay that much for a tree?"

Ellie wasn't at all sure her parents would spend a dollar for the tree, or even whether they had decided to not have a tree "for the duration." But she had promised Jimmy, so she hoped they would get one, especially with Jimmy coming home to surprise them.

The days ticked by until it was the night before school let out for the holidays.

"Get your snow gear, Peanut," said Pop after supper. "We're going for the tree tonight."

Ellie's breath left frozen feathers in the air as she and Pop walked to Corsiglia's. The stars glittered like faraway ice crystals. A fairytale sort of night.

Being alone with Pop always made Ellie feel tongue-tied. He wasn't much of a talker, and Ellie couldn't think of a thing to say. For once, Corsiglia's loudspeaker was silent. Only their boots crunching through the snow broke the stillness. At last they pushed open the market door, bells jingling from the door spring.

"What brings you out on so cold a night?" called Mr. Corsiglia from behind the cash register.

"Christmas tree," said Pop.

The grocer smiled, flashing a gold tooth. "Every year this one comes with her big brother to pick the Christmas tree. You carry on without him, no?"

Ellie nodded.

"You go ahead and look at the trees. Lorenzo," Mr. Corsiglia shouted toward the back room for his teenage son. "Go out front and help Mr. McKelvey pick one out."

"No need," said Pop. "Had my eye on one already." He strode outside, right to Ellie's tree, the tall spruce.

How did he know which tree? Ellie marveled.

"This one," he called to Mr. Corsiglia, who stood shivering in the doorway. "How much?"

Ellie cringed. Pop wasn't going to pay a buck for a tree.

"One a-dollar," Mr. Corsiglia sang out.

"Sold," said Pop, digging his worn wallet from his pants pocket.

Ever-thrifty Pop had spent a whole dollar on a tree! Ellie marveled as she trailed Pop and Lorenzo Corsiglia home, her beautiful spruce on their shoulders.

"Hot chocolate?" Pop asked after they propped the tree on the back stoop. "Green's?"

"Swell." Ellie couldn't have been more surprised if Pop had suggested dropping in on the Roosevelts at the White House. How did he know about going to Green's?

"I'll Be Home for Christmas" on the jukebox greeted Ellie and Pop at Green's, the aroma of vanilla, fudge, and magazine ink tickling Ellie's nose.

"Good evening." Miss Ruthie quickly shoved a copy of *Screen Stars* beneath the fountain counter.

"Do you have hot chocolate?" Pop asked as he helped Ellie out of her jacket and unzipped his own.

"It's powdered, but we have it," said Miss Ruthie.

"Two, please," said Pop. "With whipped cream. We'll be in a booth."

How did Pop know I like whipped cream and sitting in a booth? Ellie wondered.

Ellie didn't have to worry about making conversation. Miss Ruthie, who was usually as animated as a pencil eraser, chattered away as she made their chocolate.

"I don't know why Poppa keeps the place open on weeknights in the winter," she said. "You folks are the first I've had after supper all week. Now, summer, that's a different story." Goodness, but Miss Ruthie was on a talking jag.

Ellie was only half listening when she heard ". . . and that's why I'm joining the WAVES come the new year."

"That's brave of you, Miss Ruthie," said Pop. "Ever been away from home?"

"No," Miss Ruthie admitted. "I hear they send girls all over the country. California and Washington, D.C., and New York City. Basic training is at a college in New York City." Her eyes sparkled the way Jimmy's had.

She wanted to see the world. Like Jimmy.

Miss Ruthie brought their chocolate, then went back to *Screen Stars*, reading as she filled the soda-straw canisters. Ellie sipped slowly, savoring the dark sweetness and the warmth of the thick ironstone mug.

"You know," said Pop, stirring the whipped cream into his chocolate, "I taught Jimmy everything he knows about Christmas trees. Before you and Sal were born."

"Really?" Ellie always assumed that nothing important happened before she was born.

"Yep. Then Sal came along, and it was the three of us going to Corsiglia's."

Ellie couldn't imagine Sal getting sap on her mittens, tree needles poking her in the face.

"So how did Jimmy and I wind up getting the tree?"

Pop traced invisible circles on the scarred tabletop. "Jimmy was in junior high when you were born. He thought you were the cutest thing. Took you with him every-where."

"What about Sal? Did he take her everywhere when she was a baby?"

"They're seven years apart, and Jimmy was too young to appreciate a baby sister. She drove him crazy, tagging after him." Pop studied his thumbs. "Truth be known, Peanut, I think she's kinda jealous of how close you and Jimmy are."

Jealous? Ellie watched the snow drift across the street, piling up around a fire hydrant. Could it be that Sal was the envious one? No. Not possible.

"I always did wonder," Pop said, as if talking to himself, "why Sal stopped helping with the tree."

Ellie jerked her attention back to the table. "Sal? Help? That's a laugh." She had *never* wondered why her sister didn't help. That's just the way things were. Ellie and Jimmy did the dirty work—hauling the decorations from the attic, untangling the lights, climbing up and down the ladder, hanging ornaments, arranging tinsel just so. Sal was always someplace else, out with her goony pals or polishing her toenails.

"Maybe," Pop mused, "Sal thought two was company, three's a crowd." Before Ellie could tell him that he was barking up the wrong tree, Pop asked, "You putting the tree up Christmas Eve?"

"Sure."

"By yourself?"

"By myself." *Except that Jimmy will be home by then, and we can put it up together, just like always.*

"I know you and Jimmy always did it by yourselves," Pop said. "But it's going to be twice the work without him. How about I lend a hand this year?"

Ellie shook her head. "The fun part is when you and Mom come in to see it, and ooh and aah, and tell us how this year's tree is the best ever."

"Well, I'll set it up in the stand for you, and then it's all yours." There was a long silence, broken only by the sound of Miss Ruthie riffling the pages of her magazine. Pop seemed to be waiting for Ellie to say something, but what?

Finally, Pop glanced at his watch. "We need to head for the barn, Peanut. School night, you know." He helped Ellie on with her jacket.

"Good night, Miss Ruthie," Ellie called. Ruthie waggled her fingers without looking up from *Screen Stars*. "If I don't see you, good luck with the WAVES."

As they crossed the street, Ellie had to ask, "How did you know which tree I wanted, and that I like whipped cream on my chocolate and the booths better than the counter?"

"Easy, Peanut," Pop said with a rare smile. "Sal would've picked that tree. And she likes whipped cream, and sitting in booths, too."

12

"Forty hours to Christmas," Ellie chanted. "Thirty-nine hours and fifty-nine minutes. Thirty-nine hours and fifty-eight minutes. Thirty-nine hours—"

"Can it, Ellie." Stan cut her off. "We still have to get through a whole day of school."

"Half day," Ellie reminded him as they walked the last block to school. "We get out at noon."

The schoolyard vibrated with anticipation. Kids ran from the girls' side to the boys', teachers trying to herd them to their separate areas.

Jellyneck skidded into the crowd, hair every which way, shoelaces trailing, shirttails dangling beneath his thin jacket.

"Look who I've got!" he crowed. Behind him stood a soldier, spit-and-polish in his uniform, making Jellyneck look even messier than usual.

"Hi, Orrie," said Stan. "How's tricks in the Army?"

"There's a war on, kid." Orrie grinned and Ellie could see the Army had fixed his chipped and missing teeth. He didn't at all resemble the big-eared, slump-shouldered kid who couldn't hit the porch with their newspaper. He looked older, taller, and almost . . . well, handsome. Ellie could see why Sal and her pals went all silly about men in uniform.

"He came in last night, all the way from Fort Dix, New Jersey." Jellyneck made New Jersey sound as far away as Timbuktu.

"How long are you staying?" Ellie asked.

Orrie frowned. "Seven hours by train each way don't leave a lot of time on a two-day pass. I have to leave right after Christmas dinner."

"That's too bad." Ellie tried to figure how long it would take to come from South Carolina . . . and couldn't. She remembered Mom saying that sometimes the passenger trains got sidetracked by the ones carrying troops. It could take two days for a train to get from Fort Jackson to the Union Station on Liberty Avenue.

The first bell shrilled, shocking the rowdy schoolyard into echoing silence. Kids divided into their march-in lines, one for the boys, one for the girls.

"See you at noon, kiddo," Orrie said, socking his brother in the arm.

"Yessir," said Jellyneck, firing off a snappy salute.

"See ya later, general," Stan called over his shoulder.

The day started with the Christmas assembly. Miss Deetch read "The Night Before Christmas" as she did every year, somehow making it sound as serious as the Bible. Mrs. Miller played the piano while everyone sang Christmas carols.

Then, just in case anyone had forgotten about the war, a song for each branch of service. "From the Halls of Montezuma" for the Marines. "Anchors Aweigh" for the Navy. "Off We Go into the Wild Blue Yonder" for the Air Corps. "The Caissons Go Rolling Along" for the Army. What the heck is a caisson? Ellie wondered, as she always did.

Usually everyone got so carried away on these songs, they shouted the words. But today, the singing was quieter, subdued. All around her, Ellie heard kids sniffling, trying not to cry. Because their fathers and brothers, uncles and cousins wouldn't be home for Christmas. She felt sorry for them, but she couldn't help thinking, Jimmy will be here soon. Maybe by the time school lets out.

After assembly, the sixth grade trooped back to class, where they proceeded to do absolutely nothing for the rest of the day. For the first time, there was no class Christmas party. The sixth graders had decided to buy presents for the fighting men instead of exchanging grab-bag gifts. Without the party and gift exchange, there was nothing to do. Even Miss Granberry knew it was hopeless to try any sort of schoolwork.

"Class, you may have free time at your desks. You may talk as long you aren't too loud," she said. "If you insist on being disruptive, I'm sure I can find an arithmetic drill." With that, she commenced grading papers.

"Anybody gotten a letter lately?" Stan asked quietly.

Ellie had, but it wasn't one to share with anyone else. Unusually somber for Jimmy, full of advice—be a good girl, help Mom and Pop, remember to pray for him. It didn't sound like the kind of letter you sent someone you would see soon. Ellie knew he was just pretending that he wasn't coming home . . . but it bothered her just the same.

Victoria looked up from her Nancy Drew book. "I got a letter from my brother Buddy last week," she said. "With Christmas and all, I forgot about it." She hesitated. "Are you sure you want me to read this? It's, uh . . . different."

"Sure we're sure," Stan insisted. "Read it."

"Okay," said Victoria.

Hi Sis,

It's turkey time back home, isn't it? I don't think we're getting any bird and cranberries here, but there's lots to be thankful for. Like living, for instance. Something happened yesterday, maybe I shouldn't tell you about it, but I got to tell somebody and I don't want to fret the folks. I know I can count on you. We got this new guy from Tennessee, a kid. He said he's seventeen, but he has the face of a fifteen-year-old. I bet he lied on his service papers. He had some goofy name we couldn't remember, so we just called him

Tennessee. A big, old country boy, right out of boot camp, who'd never been anywhere or seen anything. He thought everything was just the most amazing thing he'd ever seen. Until he joined the Marines, he'd never ridden in a car or seen a movie or talked on a telephone. When they found out that Tennessee had never seen a movie, some of the guys showed him their pinup pictures, and told him that they were their girlfriends. Like these lunks could land a girl like Betty Grable or Lana Turner! You know what? He believed them!

So last night, after dinner, we're in front of the mess tent, having a smoke. Tennessee is talking a blue streak about how different this island is from the Smoky Mountains, when he spots this plane. One little old plane all by itself in the evening sky. "Looky there," he says. "A plane." He waves at the plane, since I guess that's something else he never saw before the Marines either.

But then the plane dips low and heads right for us, and I see it's a Jap Zero. I yell "Run, run, it's the Japs!" But by now, the plane is strafing us, bullets flying through the dirt. I hit the ground and curse. Pray some, too. After a while the plane goes away and I get up. But Tennessee doesn't. That nice, dumb boy from Tennessee who had never been anywhere or seen anything is dead.

He'd been in the war one whole day.

The room grew still until the whole class had gathered around Victoria, listening, barely breathing. Ralph broke the silence.

"Wow," he said. "And he didn't even get to kill anybody first."

"Shut up," Victoria snapped. She thumped open her Nancy Drew.

"What's biting her?" asked Stan. "I thought it was a swell letter."

Ellie knew what was biting Victoria, because she was thinking the same thing.

Tennessee could've been my brother.

13

"Christmas Eve is the longest day of the year." Ellie knelt on newspapers in the basement, polishing the good silver. "Nothing but a lot of cleaning and waiting for tomorrow."

"Poor you," said Sal. "At least you don't have to iron the world's biggest tablecloth and umpteen napkins." She squinted at the ironing board.

"Toots told Mom not to go to a lot of extra bother for her friends, but you know Mom." Ellie dug fingers into the jar of gritty silver polish and rubbed it into the cake server. "Company means good silver and good china and the good linen tablecloth."

The girls worked on in silence, save for the *thump whish sigh* of the steam iron. Ellie's heart jumped whenever the doorbell rang. *Jimmy!*

But it was always someone else.

Twirl-twirl. Twirl-twirl. The doorbell again.

Mom shouted down the cellar steps, "Somebody answer that. I'm up to my elbows in pie dough."

"I will." Ellie swiped her hands on the seat of her dungarees as she charged up the stairs.

Through the door glass, she saw Mr. Carlson, the postman, with a parcel in his arms.

"Looks like Jim sent you folks season's greetings," he said, handing Ellie the package. "You're lucky. The Gandecks haven't heard from three of their boys in a couple of weeks. They're worried sick."

"Really?" said Ellie.

"Yep. I'd be worried, too, with two of them over in the Pacific. Mighty bad fighting over there last month. On the other hand, you never can tell about mail in wartime. Might take months to get here, might take weeks. No rhyme or reason to it a'tall. Lucky for yunz, Jim's stateside. Well, Merry Christmas," he called as he went on his way.

"Whatcha got there?" asked Aunt Toots, whirling by with a feather duster.

"Box from Jimmy," Ellie said.

"Bless his heart," said Toots, from a cloud of dust and feathers. "Thinking of us when he's got so much on his mind."

Ellie was putting the final touches to her polishing when Mom called, "Almost three o'clock, girls. Time for the President's Christmas speech. You can finish later."

Pop tuned in the station from his Morris chair. Mom leaned forward in her armchair rocker, as if she wanted to crawl into the radio. Sal and Toots shared the sofa, with Ellie on the floor hugging her knees.

President Roosevelt called his radio speeches "fireside chats" because he liked to imagine his listeners sitting by their own fireplaces. The glowing orange radio dial and the President's friendly voice warmed Ellie as if she *were* sitting before a fireplace.

"My friends . . ." the President began, as always. He made Ellie feel he really *was* her friend.

Tonight, the President spoke about going to a place called Tehran to talk with other leaders about the war.

American boys are fighting today . . .

The President's sons were overseas, too. Did he worry they wouldn't come home?

Fighting for the thing for which they struggle.

Newsreel pictures flickered through Ellie's head. Refugees trudging the roads of Europe because their homes were gone. Germans shouting *"Sieg heil!"* at Nazi rallies. Ships burning at Pearl Harbor.

And we ask that God receive and cherish those who have given their lives, and that He keep them in honor and in the grateful memory of their countrymen forever.

Ellie gazed around at her family, heads bowed, hands clasped as if in prayer. Maybe they were.

God bless all of you who fight our battles on this Christmas Eve.

God bless us all. Keep us strong in our faith that we fight for a better day for humankind—here and everywhere.

"Amen," Mom whispered.

"Amen," Aunt Toots agreed, in her barnyard voice.

Everyone sat in silence, gazing at the radio. The room felt cold and empty without the President's warm voice.

Finally, Mom got to her feet. "I have to check on those pies."

"Wow," said Sal. "I feel like I've been to church already. Can we skip—?"

"No," said Mom and Pop together. "We are going to midnight service, and that's that."

Ellie hugged her knees closer. "Fight for a better day," the President had said. Well, her better day was coming today! Tonight!

Tonight, when Jimmy arrived.

"Sure you want to tackle this?" Pop looked from Ellie to the big spruce he had just anchored in the Christmas tree stand.

Although Ellie said, "I'm sure," she really wasn't. So much to do. Strings of lights to test. Tinsel and ornaments to hang. And at the very top of the tree, the big tin star Jimmy had made in school metal shop.

Pop was right. A lot of work for one person.

Ellie toiled up and down the stairs from the attic with box after box of ornaments. Whenever she passed her bedroom, the door was closed. Sal was probably wrapping presents.

On her last trip, the door stood ajar. Sal sprawled on the bed, surrounded by tissue-wrapped gifts. "Bringing down the decorations?" she called out.

"What do you think?" Ellie snapped.

Sal raised an angora-socked foot and traced circles in the air. "This gives you slender ankles."

Ellie thought of saying that Sal's ankles needed all the help they could get, but she didn't.

Instead, she asked, "Do you want to help decorate the tree? Not that I really need help," she added in an offhand way.

For an instant, Ellie glimpsed pure happiness on her sister's face. So! thought Ellie. Pop was right. Sal *had* felt left out all those years.

Ellie's face must have betrayed what she was thinking, because Sal quickly rearranged her expression to one of indifference.

"Might as well." Sal swung her feet to the floor and felt around for her saddle shoes. "Toots will have nine kinds of fits if we don't have a tree for her friends tomorrow."

"Okay," said Ellie, as if she, too, couldn't care less.

"Here, give me some of those boxes." Sal lifted two from Ellie's stack. "You're going to break your neck, and the ornaments too, carrying a load like that."

The McKelvey Christmas Truce had begun.

"Can't you walk a little faster?" Ellie urged Sal. St. Matthew's was only two blocks away, but a frigid wind blew straight through her skirt. Her legs were freezing, but you didn't wear snow pants to church, even for a midnight service.

"No." Sal's teeth chattered. "Not without breaking an arm on the ice. What are you complaining about? At least you're wearing kneesocks."

Feeling guilty, Ellie matched her pace to Sal's. She knew how cold Sal was. She had watched her put on her "stockings in a bottle"—leg makeup—and draw a stocking seam up the back of her leg with eyebrow pencil.

Aunt Toots strode past, spraying slushy snow in her wake. Not caring how she looked, Toots wore heavy cotton hose. "Get a move on, girls. This ain't nothing. Why, back home—"

"Yeah, yeah, we know, you walked five miles to school in snow over your head," muttered Sal.

Ellie surveyed the clear, moonless sky. There was her old friend the North Star, shining especially bright tonight. *Follow it home, Jimmy. And hurry! It's almost Christmas Day.*

On the church steps, Ellie spied Jellyneck and his whole family. A Jelinek or two turned up on Sunday sometimes, but all nine of them plus their mother? And wearing new coats? Mrs. Jelinek had a new hat as well.

Jellyneck sidled over in the icy vestibule. "Hey, Ellie, look." He held out his arms for inspection. "Orrie took us shopping and we all got new coats. How about them apples?"

"Pretty swell apples," she agreed.

"Merry Christmas," he said with a broad smile as they filed into the rapidly filling sanctuary.

I'm happy for him, Ellie told herself.

But as she watched the flickering altar candles, Ellie asked God to forgive her for being jealous of Jellyneck. Because his brother sat next to him tonight.

14

ick tick tick. Ellie picked up the clock and peered at the eerie, glowing green hands and numbers. Two-fifteen. Sighing, she plunked it back on her bedside table, with a little *ping* of the alarm.

"Cut it out, Ellie." Sal heaved a pillow at her. "That's the four-hundredth time you've looked at that clock. Anybody would think you still believe in Santa Claus."

"You cut it out." Ellie threw the pillow back. She looked at the clock. Again.

Two-twenty.

"Sal? You asleep?"

"What do you think?" Sal sounded grouchy.

"Do you remember the year that we saw Santa Claus?"

"Santa Claus, my foot. You know good and well that was Jimmy dressed up in a Santa suit." *Sca-reech* Sal's bedsprings sang as she sat up. "He was in a play at the high school, and he wore his costume home to surprise us."

"I know." Ellie turned toward her sister's bed. "But we *thought* it was Santa."

"Maybe *you* thought it was Santa." Sal didn't sound grouchy anymore. "Ellie?"

"Hmmm?"

"You don't think, I mean, you don't really believe . . ." Sal took a deep breath. "You know Jimmy can't come home for Christmas," she finished in a rush. "Don't you?"

"Fat lot you know." As soon as she said it, Ellie wished she hadn't.

Rustle screech rustle from the other bed. *Click.* Sal snapped on her bedside lamp.

"Hey, what's the big idea?" Ellie threw an arm over her eyes.

"The big idea is that there is no way he can get all the way from South Carolina on a two-day pass, which is all they are granting these days. Mom and Pop are going to be sad enough this Christmas without you drooping around. I miss him, too, but there isn't anything we can do about it."

"But he *is* coming," Ellie insisted. "He'll find a way. I know it."

"My sister, the Gypsy fortune-teller," Sal snorted. "Do you think he's keeping this all a big fat secret? That he's going to drop out of the sky just in time for Christmas dinner?" She clicked off the lamp.

That was exactly what Ellie thought. She waited a minute, then said, "Jimmy said to keep the tree up, that he'd be home."

But Sal had already gone back to sleep, gently whistling through her nose.

Ellie stared at the shadows the dimmed streetlights cast on the ceiling. She pulled the pillow over her head, but "I'll Be Home for Christmas" sang on in her mind. Bing Crosby, of course.

"You kids get away from that tree," Mom said, as she did every year. "No presents until after breakfast."

But this year, there was no Jimmy to wheedle "Aw, Ma. Just one little present before breakfast?" He would open the biggest present under the tree, then so would Sal and Ellie, and before long, everyone would have forgotten about breakfast.

Without Jimmy, Sal and Ellie ate Christmas breakfast for the first time in their lives. And for the first time, Mom plunked the Shredded Wheat box on the table, along with the milk bottle, and announced, "I only have the strength to cook one big meal today." Shredded Wheat had never seemed less appetizing to Ellie.

Breakfast finally over, Pop turned on the radio, spinning the dial, looking for holiday music.

"I'll be home for Christ . . ." Bing boomed into the room. Again.

"Pop, could you find another station, please?" said Ellie.

Her father fiddled with the knobs until he came to the voice of an unfamiliar newscaster.

"Ah, but there is no peace on earth today, my listeners," the announcer said in a lugubrious voice.

"Why don't we put some records on?" asked Toots, raising the record player lid. The first notes of "Winter Wonderland" filled the living room.

The parcel from South Carolina stood like a brown boulder beneath the tree, its twine and heavy paper wrappings wildly out of place amid the red and green tissue-wrapped gifts.

"Let's bust into Jimmy's box, whaddya say?" Toots whipped a jackknife from her dungarees pocket and commenced sawing away at the binding twine.

Ellie thought they should wait for Jimmy, but she knew she should keep her thoughts to herself.

Once the box was open, Mom took over. Burrowing through crumpled wads of South Carolina newspapers, she dug out smaller packages, each neatly wrapped in more newspaper. Ellie fidgeted, twisting a strand of tinsel around her finger, as Mom handed first Pop, then Toots, their gifts. Pop's gift was a book, *See Here, Private Hargrove*.

"I've heard this book is funny," Pop said. "Written by an Army fella about being in boot camp."

Toots shook something silky from her wrappings.

"I'll be," she exclaimed. "Wouldja look at this." She waved a large, flat square of satin printed with eagles, the American flag, and Uncle Sam shaking a soldier's hand. Above the scene were the words "Greetings from Fort Jackson, South Carolina."

"What is it?" Ellie asked, reaching over to twiddle the gold fringe trim.

"It's a pillowcase," said Toots, smoothing the satin across her lap. "Not a sleeping pillow," she added, catching Ellie's incredulous look. "You stuff it with rags and put it on your bed for decoration."

"Here you go." Mom passed Sal a large flat parcel. Ellie watched her sister peel layer after layer of newspaper, the size of the gift steadily shrinking. Finally, Sal pulled away the last of the paper to reveal a picture frame.

Ha! thought Ellie. That's not such a great gift!

A note was taped to the glass, in the blank picture space.

For Sal, Queen of the Freshman Class.

The guys in my barracks have been ribbing me about my Lana picture. Not Lana, but her frame. We don't have bureaus or dressers in boot camp, just foot-lockers. Lana and her frame is what they call "non-regulation." I remember that your Sinatra pic could use a better home. So use this for old Frankie, until Lana and I come home.

Your brother,
Jimmy (aka Doc)

"This will look nice on my dresser." Sal ran her fingers over the glass. "For the duration."

"For you, Ellie," Mom said, handing her something light and flat. Why, it was the exact size and shape for a box of . . .

"Nylons!" shrieked Sal. "*Nobody* can get nylons anymore. I hate you!"

"What was Jimmy thinking?" Mom said, downright shocked.

"Maybe he got the boxes mixed up," said Sal. "I'm older."

Ellie pulled out a folded sheet of stationery and read:

Dear Movie Star,

Sal will probably say I mixed up the boxes and that these stockings are hers. Well, they aren't. You'll be going to junior high next year, and that was when Sal got her first pair. The PX is about the only place you can still buy them, so these are for you. Save them for a special occasion, OK? I know you will look as beautiful as Betty Grable. Lana is beautiful, but Betty has the best legs!

Merry Christmas, Jimmy

P.S. Ask Mom or Sal how you hold these things up! There's a limit to what a fella can buy at the PX without getting funny looks.

Ellie looked down at her shapeless legs. Maybe some day they *would* be as beautiful as Betty Grable's. Maybe.

Meanwhile, Mom was opening her present. "Oh, my," she breathed. In her lap lay a formal color-tinted portrait of Jimmy in dress uniform.

Ellie moved in for a closer look. The soldier in the picture was handsome, but he didn't look like Jimmy. The photographer had colored the eyes the wrong color blue, a sort of navy, instead of Jimmy's blue, like the sky and the sea mixed together. And Jimmy's hair was auburn, not brick red.

But the colors didn't bother Ellie as much as the soldier's expression. Unsmiling, and Jimmy always smiled. And his eyes . . . the eyes looked as if they saw something that no one else could. Solemn eyes.

The picture reminded Ellie of the ones on Miss Granberry's wall. She shivered.

"Merry Christmas, kiddo." Toots handed Ellie a flat packet with "Do Not Open Until Christmas" stickers plastered all over it. Sal was tearing into an identical packet.

"Wow," enthused Sal. "A war bond."

"You shouldn't have," said Mom. "Eighteen dollars and seventy-five cents is a lot of money."

Toots shrugged. "Hey, it's for the war effort. Just a little something for the future. In ten years they can cash it in for twenty-five dollars."

Ellie couldn't imagine so much money, either now or in ten years. "Gee, thanks, Toots," was all she could manage.

"And that ain't all," said Toots as she rooted through the gifts still under the tree. She emerged with two wrapped packages that were unmistakably books. Ellie peeled back the tissue. It was a book all right.

"*Norma Kent of the WACs*," she read aloud. The last thing Ellie wanted to read right now was a book about a member of the Women's Army Corps.

"*Gone with the Wind*," chirped Sal. "Swell, Aunt Toots! That was a terrific movie, and now I can read the story over and over." Ellie peered over Sal's shoulder as she riffled the pages. It was long, but it looked a lot better than *Norma Kent*.

"Thanks, Toots," Ellie said, remembering her manners. "This is for you," she added, handing her aunt her gift.

Toots started to rip into the lumpy-looking parcel.

"Careful," said Mom. "We can use that paper again next year."

"Sorry," said Toots, carefully prying off the stickers. "Wow! Bed socks. Just what I need when I get in that freezing bed every morning." She fit the socks over her hands, and waved them in the air. "Thanks, Short Stuff."

"You're welcome," said Ellie. She tossed an identical lumpy package into Sal's lap.

"Gee," said Sal. "I wonder what *this* could be?"

No one mentioned that Army green was a strange color for bed socks. The same color as the scarf in the last package under the tree.

Jimmy's scarf.

"Sal, Toots, I need you in the kitchen," Mom said, piling the gift-wrappings on the sofa. "Ellie, why don't you redd up in here? You can smooth out the tissue for next year."

That suited Ellie just fine. She would be the first to see Jimmy get off the streetcar.

"Toots, what time are your friends coming?" Ellie called out to the kitchen.

"I told them any time after four," Toots shouted back.

At three, Ellie took up watch at the front door. The Number 10 lumbered to a stop, disgorging a gaggle of girls. Ellie watched them pick their way up the street to the terrace steps. These had to be Toots's work pals. No men. No Jimmy. She opened the storm door, frosty air swirling up and under her dress.

"Hey, kid, is this the McKelveys'?" called one of the girls from the bottom porch step, squinting at a scrap of paper in her gloved hand.

"Yep," said Ellie.

"This is the place then," said another girl in a purple coat with a fake fox collar. The girls stomped up the front steps, shaking the snow from their boots.

"Company's here," Ellie shouted in the direction of the kitchen.

Toots hustled into the entryway, Mom and Sal on her heels. Toots introduced everyone around, and it seemed to Ellie they were all named Betty.

"We was so scared of bein' late, we're kinda early," said a redheaded Betty. "Sorry, ma'am."

"Nonsense," said Mom with a dismissive wave of her hand. "Who wants to spend Christmas in a boarding-house?"

"Thanks, Mrs. McKelvey," said fake-fox Betty. "Swell of you to invite us."

"Our pleasure," said Mom.

After the guests had offered to help in the kitchen and she had refused, Mom added "Please make yourselves at home while I finish up the meal."

They did. Toots put on Glenn Miller records, and the Bettys jitterbugged, coming perilously close to the Christmas tree. Ellie knelt on the sofa, watching for the Number 10 from the window. The mohair upholstery prickled her knees, but she didn't budge.

Jimmy wasn't on the next streetcar. Or the next. Or the one after that.

"Supper is almost ready," Mom called from the dining room. "Would you girls like to freshen up? Toots, show them the washroom."

The girls clattered upstairs, leaving Ellie hanging over the sofa back, staring out the window, willing Jimmy's streetcar to arrive.

Swish creak. The kitchen door.

"Ellie, what are you doing?" said Mom. "I need you in the kitchen." *Swish creak.* She was gone.

Like magic, the Number 10 rattled into view. *Oh please oh please oh please.*

Upstairs, giggling and voices and the bathroom door slamming.

"You girls ready?" Mom called up. "Sounds like a lot of horsing around up there."

"Yes ma'am sister dear," Toots hollered down.

The streetcar door opened as Ellie held her breath. One person. One single person.

A man.

The snow cleared for a moment, and Ellie glimpsed copper-colored hair. A leather jacket. A familiar slouch of the shoulders.

Ellie flew out the door without stopping for a coat. Skidding sideways down the terrace, snow filled her Mary Janes, the wind knifed through her skirts. Ellie didn't care.

"Jimmy!" she screamed.

A pair of leather-clad arms reached out and steadied her as she slid on the pavement.

"Hold on there," said a stranger's voice. "I don't know who you are, but I'm not Jimmy."

15

Ellie peered at the stranger through the stinging snow. Her face burned as she remembered that Jimmy's old leather jacket was upstairs in his closet.

"Where's your coat?" asked the stranger. Close up, Ellie could see he was younger than Jimmy, closer to Toots's age. "Where did you come from?"

"Across the street." She hugged her elbows against the icy wind.

"The one with the service flag? Is that where Toots Guilfoyle lives?"

"Yep," said Ellie, trying to keep her teeth from chattering.

"Then you would be Ellie. I'm Wally Brown." He started to offer his hand, then shook his head. "What am I thinking? You must be freezing. What say we make for the house?"

Wally took Ellie's arm as they crossed the street. Did she detect a limp in his step?

Toots met them on the terrace steps and took Wally's other arm.

"What do you think I am?" Wally pretended to be insulted. "A ninety-pound weakling?"

"Heck, no." Toots propelled him up the steps. "Didn't want you bending Ellie's ear while we're all starving."

As he moved past, Ellie spied a metal brace clamped to Wally's left shoe. He caught her glance.

"Polio," he said as he handed her his jacket in the entry. "I'm lucky. Some kids I knew in the hospital never walked again. Some of them wound up in an iron lung because they couldn't breathe on their own. Me, I just have a little old limp and a leg brace. Now you know why I'm 4-F."

"Ellie," Mom scolded. "I hope you haven't been asking our guest rude questions."

"Not at all, Mrs. McKelvey." Wally handed Mom a small package. "Homemade fudge, courtesy of my mom and sister back home in Erie."

Ellie's mouth watered, remembering the last time she made candy. Jimmy trying to spoon up the fudge before it had set. Sal slapping his hand away.

He'll be here. Soon.

All through turkey and dressing and cranberries, Ellie couldn't help thinking Jimmy should be here, not this Wally Brown.

"Sorry there aren't seconds," said Mom, taking the dark meat nobody else wanted.

"Are you kidding?" said a Betty. "I haven't eaten like this since I left home."

"Heck, I didn't eat like this when I *lived* at home!" joked the redheaded Betty.

For a minute Ellie thought, This is almost like the old days.

"Even if you had more, I couldn't eat another bite," Wally assured Mom.

"But there *is* more," she protested. "I have pies."

I was going to make frosted gingerbread for Jimmy. The familiar lump was back in Ellie's throat and growing bigger by the minute.

"Should we loosen our belts a spell before tackling dessert?" asked Pop.

"Good idea," said Toots. "Anybody want to play Hearts?"

"Go ahead," Ellie told Sal. "I'll help Mom redd up the kitchen."

"Are you sure?" Sal gave her sister a suspicious look.

"Sure." Ellie shrugged. "It's Christmas."

"Thanks, Peanut," Sal said. "I owe you."

It seemed as if they had used every plate, pot, and pan. Just when Ellie thought she was done, Mom would say, "There's another stack of plates on the counter."

At long, long last the dishes were washed, dried, and put away, the kitchen clean.

"Let's go join the Hearts game," said Mom, heading for the living room.

Ellie dawdled over the silverware drawer. "Okay, I'll be out in a minute."

Alone in the kitchen, Ellie's throat tightened. She knew she was just a breath away from tears. But she couldn't cry, not here at least. What if somebody came out for a glass of water? She went down to the basement, where she could be alone.

Dropping to the bottom step, she buried her head in her arms and sobbed. She might have been there a minute or an hour, when the kitchen door opened.

"Ellie, is that you? Are you all right?" Wally called softly.

"Yes," Ellie hiccuped.

"You don't sound all right." *Thump clunk. Thump clunk.* Wally eased himself down next to Ellie, braced leg sticking out straight on the stairs. "Now, what's the trouble?"

Without meaning to, Ellie blubbered out the whole story. Well, almost the whole story. She left out the part about snooping in Toots's mail.

"I'm sorry," said Wally. "Bet you thought I was him when I got off the trolley."

"It's not your fault." Ellie groped her pocket for a hanky.

Wally dangled a handkerchief over her shoulder. "Go ahead. It's clean."

Ellie wiped her eyes and nose. "Jimmy always has a clean hanky when I need one."

"He must be a swell guy." Wally's voice was warm and comforting, like President Roosevelt's. "Tell me about him."

So she did. Everything she could remember. "He gave me nylons for Christmas."

Wally whistled. "You *must* be special. I know girls who would sell their grandmothers for a pair of nylons."

Ellie sniffled. "Really?"

He raised his hand. "Scout's honor. You *are* special."

"But not special enough for him to come home." Ellie's head drooped.

Wally sighed. "There's a war on, kiddo. There might be a dozen reasons why he didn't make it. None of them his fault."

"But he promised." Ellie knew she was whining and didn't care. "Jimmy always keeps his promises."

"Things don't always work out the way we want," said Wally. "Me, I wanted to join up, but the service doesn't want gimpy soldiers."

Wally cleared his throat. "Ellie, you aren't the only one wishing Jimmy were here. Sal misses him something awful. Your mom and dad, too. They're doing their darndest to give us a happy holiday, but you know they miss him, too."

From upstairs, dance music. "Sing, Sing, Sing." Sal's cheering up music.

"We're all just trying to have a merry Christmas."

Ellie hung her head. "I guess you wish you were home with your family, too."

Wally patted Ellie's arm. "True. But I'm mighty thankful to be here tonight."

"Okay, I'm better now," she said.

"That's a girl. Let's go upstairs. I think your mom is about to serve pie."

So Ellie rinsed her face in the kitchen sink, then helped Mom serve up the pumpkin pies. She listened to Toots and the Bettys tell funny stories about work, mostly about Wally, the only man in their department. Players rotated in and out of the Hearts game. And the clock ticked relentlessly toward the end of the evening.

"That's it for me," said Wally, rising from the card table.

"You're just tired of getting skunked," kidded the red-headed Betty.

"Yeah," he admitted with a grin. "But it's getting late."

Don't go, Ellie wanted to say. Because when Wally and the Bettys were gone, she would be alone with her thoughts.

The guests crowded the entry, tugging on snow boots, tying babushkas. Ellie thrust a lumpy package into Wally's hands.

"Merry Christmas," she said. "For loaning me the hanky and all."

"But this is Jimmy's," Wally protested, reading the tag.

"You take it." Ellie swallowed hard. "I can make him another one."

"Thank you." Wally opened the box, gently lifted the scarf from its tissue-paper nest, and wound it around his neck, tucking the ends into his leather jacket. He smiled crookedly. "See? I get to wear Army green after all."

Ellie stood on the icy porch, watching the Bettys and

Wally disappear into the gloom of Macken Street, trying to make Christmas last just a little longer. Finally, her numb feet and chattering teeth drove her inside. The house seemed empty without the clatter and chatter of their guests. Then, as if to fill the aching silence, everyone began to talk at once.

"Such nice girls," Mom said, stacking the dessert plates.

"Pretty swell," Sal agreed. "And that Wally wasn't so bad either."

"Kind of livened up the place." Pop settled into the Morris chair and fiddled with the radio dial. "But it'll be good to get things back to normal, with the holidays over."

Normal? What was Pop talking about? Ellie wondered. How could a house without Jimmy be normal? The tight feeling crept back into Ellie's throat.

"What a day!" Ellie faked a big yawn. "Think I'll hit the hay." She was in her pajamas and under the covers in record time. Go to sleep, she willed herself. Stop thinking and go to sleep.

But she was still awake when Sal came upstairs. Wide-eyed, she stared at the ceiling as Sal brushed her hair and creamed her face. Once in bed, Sal flounced and flipped around, pulling the quilts just so, smacking the bolster into shape. At last, Sal's breathing turned slow and even. And Ellie could cry softly into her pillow.

Jimmy, where are you?

16

Christmas had been on a Saturday, but come Sunday night, Toots went back to work, with Mom and Pop following the next morning.

"Leaving us with all the work," Sal groused. "Trust Mom to think a week off from school means we can spend a week cleaning. We might as well be under house arrest."

"Hmmm?" Ellie mumbled. She was too worried about Jimmy to care about housework or anything else—why hadn't Jimmy kept his promise? Where was he?

On New Year's Eve, Toots went out with the Bettys. Ellie started a new scarf for Jimmy. Pop read *Life* magazine while Mom searched for a good radio show. Sal skulked from room to room, pouting because Mom wouldn't let her go to Connie Cavendish's party.

"Fourteen isn't old enough for night parties and dates," Mom said.

"I am sooo mortified," Sal moaned over and over. "Everyone will be there."

"Everyone but you," Mom said. "Maybe next year."

Sal rolled her eyes. "Like anyone will invite me."

"Fred will invite you. He asked you this time," Ellie reminded her.

"Oh, *him*." Sal dismissed the Western Union boy with a hand flick. "He's *such* a drip."

"Yeah, but he *does* have a uniform," Ellie pointed out. "I thought Connie Cavendish liked men in uniforms."

"Can the drama, Greta Garbo," Mom said. "Make yourself useful. Why don't you and Ellie take down the tree?"

"No!" Ellie shouted. Then, more calmly, "I promised Jimmy we'd leave the tree up until he comes home."

"The tree will dry out," Mom said. "It could catch fire."

"But I promised," Ellie repeated.

Pop looked up from his *Life* magazine. "I think we can keep the tree up a while longer. That is, if Ellie agrees to water it."

Mom frowned. "But it's dangerous."

"So we'll take the lights off," said Pop. "And none of us smokes."

"Thanks, Pop." Ellie hugged him.

"After all, Peanut, we paid a whole dollar for this fine tree." Pop gave her a wink.

Ellie carefully unwound the lights from around the ornaments. *Don't worry, Tree. You're staying up until Jimmy comes home. Whenever that is.*

———

Ellie started back to school the dreary first week of January. One week went by, then two, and there was no letter from Jimmy.

Again, Ellie trekked home at lunch to check the mail. The icy wind bored through her coat; slush seeped through her worn galoshes. Who cared? How could she sit in school all afternoon not knowing if there was a letter?

But there never was.

Ellie wasn't the only one going home for lunch.

Victoria did, too.

Every noon, they slogged up the hill to the corner where Victoria turned left, Ellie right.

Ellie figured Victoria must be looking for a letter, too, but didn't know for sure, because they never talked. If Victoria wasn't speaking first, Ellie wasn't either. The walk was long; the only sound was the *scrunch scrunch* of their boots in the snow. Still, Ellie knew that Victoria had not gone home for lunch before this. Furthermore, she remembered what Mr. Carlson had said at Christmastime, that the Gandecks hadn't heard from their boys in a while.

The third week of January began with bright blue skies so cold, it hurt to breathe. Sun glared on the snow. Ellie kept her head down against the painful brightness as she started home at noon. Left boot, right boot, *scrunch scrunch*.

"You heard from Jimmy?"

Ellie thought she must be hearing things—it couldn't be Victoria speaking to her.

"Well, have you?"

It was Victoria, all right.

"No."

"Us either. Three of the boys haven't written. Scary, ain't it?"

Was this some kind of trick? But Victoria sounded as worried as Ellie.

"Yes, it's scary. How long since you heard?"

"Thanksgiving." Victoria's voice stretched thin, as if she might cry. "You?"

"Jimmy sent Christmas presents."

"Lucky duck."

Behind them, a car labored uphill, snow chains jangling. A decrepit Ford, an ancient man hunched over the wheel, wheezed and coughed past them.

"He's got a 'C' gas sticker," Ellie observed. "He doesn't look like a doctor."

Victoria took a sharp breath. "That's old man Wheeler," she said. "He's the weekday Western Union man."

Scrunchscrunchscrunch. The girls moved as fast as their clumsy boots allowed.

The car clanked on and on. Past the Jelineks'. The Schmidts'. The Hales'.

The Ford halted at the alley between Ellie's house and Victoria's, tailpipe billowing clouds of exhaust.

The girls froze. *Ohpleaseohpleaseohpleaseno,* Ellie whispered to herself.

Then the Ford turned left and rolled to a stop in front of

the Gandecks'. Ellie let out a whoosh of relief, leaving a cloud of frozen vapor in the air.

Victoria stood rooted to the sidewalk, her face bone-white.

"C'mon," urged Ellie. "I'll come with you."

Victoria didn't move.

"Come *on*." Ellie grabbed Victoria's mittened hand and dragged her the last block. Closer, she could see old man Wheeler on the porch, Mrs. Gandeck holding the yellow telegram. *Dear God, I'm sorry for every mean thing I thought about Victoria.*

Victoria shook free of Ellie and stumbled up the porch steps. "Who is it, Ma?" she asked in a strangled voice. "Which one?"

Mrs. Gandeck was laughing and crying at the same time. "Buddy." Sobs. Laughter.

"Is he . . . ?" Victoria choked out.

"He's in a hospital in Hawaii. Thank God in Heaven, he's safe."

Ellie crept away, leaving Victoria and her mother screaming and hugging on the icy porch. Trudging up her own porch steps, she stopped to look in the mailbox before making herself a peanut butter sandwich.

The mailbox was empty.

Again.

In the next week, Ellie heard more about Buddy Gandeck than she ever wanted. I'm glad he's okay, she reminded herself. But it was tough going, with Victoria in her new role, Sister of a Hero.

"He was hurt at Tarawa," she explained at recess. "You know that island in the Pacific the Marines took at Thanksgiving? Thousands were slaughtered." Victoria savored the word "slaughtered" as if it were chocolate.

"So what happened?" asked Ralph. "Was he shot?"

"No. Something called battle fatigue. He's in a hospital in Hawaii for a rest."

How nice, Ellie thought, a sour taste in her mouth. I wish my brother could get battle fatigue and have a vacation in Hawaii.

"He got a Bronze Star. They say he was a real hero, killed a lot of Japs after everybody else he was with died."

So Victoria's brother gets a Bronze Star, Ellie brooded. And all I want is a letter from mine.

The last week of January dragged by on slushy feet, each day drearier than the one before. Ellie felt numb. Not cold numb, but inside numb. She realized that Jimmy's letters had always made her day, even the dull ones about bad food and barracks inspections. She stopped coming home for lunch and she stopped looking for the North Star.

Sal turned fifteen at the beginning of February, and started lobbying for a war job again at supper one night.

"Pleeease," she wheedled. "It's legal to work in a plant if you're fifteen. Connie Cavendish says . . ."

"If I hear one more word about Connie Cavendish,"

Mom said, "I'll set you to scrubbing out the basement . . . by yourself. Not another word!" She thumped down her teacup in the saucer so firmly that Ellie peeked to see if it had chipped.

"If you want a job," Pop said, "see if anybody in the neighborhood needs help after school. With the men gone and the young fellas working war jobs, seems to me all the shops on Macken Street are shorthanded."

"Oh, all right." Sal sighed dramatically. "I'll look. Not that I'll find anything."

Ellie poked at her bread pudding, searching for raisins. If Jimmy had been there, he would've said something funny about Sal not wanting to work where she couldn't meet boys or look glamorous. Instead, Ellie was left with the gloomy realization that if Sal got a job, Ellie got all the housework.

"He's okay, El," Stan reassured her as she shuffled through the afternoon mail one bleak day after school. Bills for Pop, letters for Toots and Sal. *Life* magazine.

"How do you know?" Ellie demanded. "You don't really know, do you?"

"Jeepers, no." Stan took a step back. "I'm just trying to be a good friend."

But you don't know. You don't know at all.

"Hello, Ellie McKelvey," Trudy sang out as Ellie stamped through the butcher shop door. "What can I do for you to-day?"

Ellie took off her damp mittens and felt her pockets for the ration books. What was Trudy so darned happy about? The sun hadn't been out in days. She hadn't heard from Jimmy in weeks and weeks. Maybe . . . had Trudy heard from him?

"Pound of ground." Ellie handed over the ration books.

Trudy sang "The Hut-Sut Song" under her breath as she slapped the meat on the scales. Ellie wondered what "ground meat" was. It wasn't hamburger, that was sure.

"So, uh, Trudy, have you heard from Jimmy lately?" Ellie tried to sound casual.

"Not since Christmas. But look at this." Trudy wiped her hands before reaching beneath the collar of her butcher's coat. A heart-shaped locket on a chain dangled from her sturdy fingers.

"Pretty," Ellie said, trying not to sound envious. "From Jimmy?"

"Mmm-hmm." Trudy tucked the locket back inside her coat. "Got it just after Thanksgiving. Said he wanted to send it early, just in case."

"In case of what?"

"In case he got shipped out, I guess." Trudy's capable hands quickly wrapped the ground meat.

Ellie took the paper parcel, and stomped out into the dreary afternoon. Her mood matched the weather.

Dark.

Then finally, one sleety day, there were letters for the McKelveys from Private James McKelvey. But not from

South Carolina. From some place called APO New York. Ellie ripped into her envelope right there on the porch, sleet pellets popping all around her.

January 21, 1944
Somewhere in England

England? But the envelope said New York.

Dear Movie Star,

Sorry I haven't written, but I couldn't tell you I was shipping out. I'm not allowed to say exactly where I am. My address is the APO Box in New York. How was Christmas on Macken Street? I hope you still have the tree up. I spent the day on a troop ship. We had turkey and the trimmings, sang carols, and that was Christmas. We got our holiday packages before we left, so me and the fellas had two Christmases, one on land and one at sea. The whole barracks sampled Toots's cookies. The boys decided those things might make good weapons, since they weighed about as much as a bomb. Just kidding . . . the cookies were swell!

Crossing the Atlantic on a troop ship ain't no Swiss picnic. It used to be an ocean liner, but the military ripped out the fancy stuff and jammed in as many hammocks as they could. Just try sleeping with some guy's behind in your face, in the hammock above you. Especially the nights we had beans, if you know what

I mean! It was so smelly that Max and me spent a lot of time topside. We would've slept up there, if it hadn't been so cold and windy. Halfway across, bad weather set in. I didn't get sick, but guys were tossing their cookies like crazy. Which didn't help the smell belowdecks. But we got here in one piece, and you can't ask for more than that, with German subs chasing us all the way over.

Love, Doc Jimmy

P.S. How did you like the stockings? Has Sal tried to snitch them yet?

Ellie's mind whirled. Jimmy was in England. He was okay. Relief!

But he said he'd be home for Christmas.

Ellie felt both happy and mad. Why couldn't she just feel all happy or all mad? Maybe this was what adults meant when they said that life wasn't simple.

Maybe being a grownup wasn't all it was cracked up to be.

17

February is the most boring month," Ellie gloomed as she slogged her way to school.

"At least it's short," Stan offered. "And almost over."

They passed Mrs. Schmidt, scrubbing her porch as she did every morning.

"Good morning, Mrs. Schmidt," they called. She looked up and waved her scrub brush.

How could your only son die, Ellie wondered, and still you scrub your porch every morning? How could she care about a porch?

"I heard Sal's got a job." Stan said. "I thought your parents didn't want her to work."

"They didn't want her working nights in a war plant," Ellie answered. "Mom says the men make it tough for her and Toots sometimes. Smart remarks and stuff."

"Really?" Stan looked interested. "What kind of stuff?"

"Mom won't say. She just said that Sal wasn't working there, 'end of discussion'."

"So how did she wind up at Green's?" asked Stan.

"When Miss Ruthie went in the WAVES, she left Mr. Green without anybody to work the after-school and weekend times when it's real busy."

"Heck, I'd work there in a minute," said Stan. "All the candy and soda you want, and you can read the comic books for free."

"That's why Mr. Green wouldn't hire anybody under fifteen." Ellie gave Stan a playful poke in the ribs. "Too much mooching."

"What does Sal do?" asked Stan. "I haven't been in since she started."

"Pretty much the same stuff Miss Ruthie did. Make sodas, scoop ice cream, run the register. Oh yeah, and talk to boys. Fred the Western Union guy hangs out there all the time, making cow eyes at her. She's like a boy magnet."

"I believe it," Stan said with a grin. "That Sal can steam your glasses!"

"Boys," Ellie snorted. "You're all alike."

"Did you get up on the wrong side of the bed?" Stan said. "Well, I know something that will cheer you up. Ma's taking the whole gang Downtown to the Paramount Saturday to see *The Fighting Sullivans*."

"Really? How come?"

"You know the *Juneau*, the boat the Sullivan brothers were on when the Japs blew it up and all five brothers died?"

"Of course." It had been big news last school year.

"That was the same boat Bill Schmidt was on."

"Yeah I know. So what?" Ellie shrugged.

"Ma thinks we should see how our street is part of history."

"So who's going?"

"Anybody who wants to."

Ellie hoped that "anybody" did not include Victoria.

"What a gyp," Ralph griped as they left the Paramount. "There wasn't hardly any war stuff in that movie. They was little kids, and then the next thing you know, they're dead. I want my money back."

"It wasn't your money," Ellie pointed out. "Mrs. Kozelle paid."

"Yeah, and Bill Schmidt wasn't in the movie, either," Victoria complained. "You said he would be." She socked Stan's arm.

"I did not," Stan said, backing away from Victoria's fist.

"Did too."

"Children!" said Mrs. Kozelle, bustling up behind them. "Manners, please! I believe the girls will sit with me on the way home."

That was how Ellie wound up squashed between Victoria and Bridget on the Number 10 going home. They chattered across Ellie's lap as if she were invisible.

Not that Ellie cared. She looked around for the boys. No sign of them in the packed car. They were probably standing down front by the motorman. She stared at Mrs.

Kozelle's head, in the seat ahead of her. She wore a clown-ish hat with a pompom on the peak. Ellie watched the pompom bob with the motion of the streetcar, and worked on making herself invisible.

"So," Bridget shouted above the streetcar din, "is Buddy going back to the Pacific? When my cousin got shot in the leg, they took the bullet out and he went right back."

"Maybe." Victoria sounded vague. "The doctors say he needs a long rest." She fiddled with her pocketbook, the subject of Buddy somehow finished. Bridget turned to Ellie.

"So, Ellie," she said, "what does Jimmy have to say?"

"Not much," Ellie said, not wanting to talk either.

"I guess not," Victoria said. "He's a *medic*." She said it the same way she'd said *slacker*. "He's too busy emptying bed-pans to write."

Ellie gripped her own pocketbook, fighting the urge to clout Victoria over the head.

The trolley toiled up Macken Street. *Clang clang.* The motorman opened the door. Ellie couldn't wait to be away from Victoria.

Stan and his mother waited for Ellie at the foot of the steps.

"Ma saw some kind of commotion at Jellyneck's when we went by," he said in a low voice. Then to everyone else, "What say we all walk Jellyneck home?" he said loudly.

"Why?" asked Ralph. "Can't he find his way by himself?"

Everyone thought that was hilarious until they saw Mrs. Kozelle steering Jellyneck down Macken Street. Silently, the gang fell in line behind them.

Crickle crackle crickle crackle. The false spring thaw over, the melted snow had refrozen. At the foot of her terrace, Mrs. Schmidt chipped at the ice with a spade. She made a quick sign of the cross as they passed. Ellie tried to walk faster, but her slick-soled Mary Janes wouldn't let her.

Crickle crackle crickle crackle. Ellie and the rest baby-stepped down the hill, arms out for balance. Past the Schmidts', Ellie saw the crowd in front of the Jelineks'. At the curb, a shiny black Packard.

"Reverend Schuyler's car," Stan muttered to Ellie. "Somebody's dead."

"Who?" The little Jelineks all had bad coughs. The older boys liked to hitch rides on freight trains and the backs of delivery trucks. Someone was always bringing Mr. Jelinek home from the Do-Drop, too drunk to walk.

Crickle crackle crickle crackle. Ellie picked out the oldest brothers in the crowd, huddled in the yard with their friends. High school boys smoking cigarettes, jacket collars around their ears. Who died? Which one?

The gang trooped up the front steps, Mrs. Kozelle and Jellyneck in the lead. Ellie remembered to avoid the broken step.

"Uh, thanks," said Jellyneck. "For the movie and all."

"Nonsense," said Mrs. Kozelle. "We're going in with you. Excuse me, gentlemen," she said to some junior high boys blocking the front door. They shuffled aside, heads down, shoulders hunched.

The stench of cigarettes and boiled cabbage and dirty diapers hit Ellie like a punch in the nose. She had known Jellyneck her whole life, and had never once been in his house. Jellyneck always met her and Stan at the door. Now she knew why.

The house was as cold as a crypt. The rooms were clean but bare. Faded, rose-patterned wallpaper, torn and hanging in spots. A single ceiling bulb with a pull chain gave the only light.

Men handed around a bottle in a brown paper bag, gulping greedily before passing it on. Someone thrust the bag in Jellyneck's face.

"Drink up, kid," said a man's voice. "You're gonna need it."

"Get away from him," Mrs. Kozelle barked, swatting away the bag.

Several little Jelineks, with runny noses and dirty faces, huddled in a corner sobbing. Mrs. Kozelle crouched to talk to them. "Where's your mother?"

"Ma's in the bedroom," the biggest one snuffled. "With the min'ster man. They said to go away."

"I'm sure they didn't mean it," said Mrs. Kozelle. "Let's go find her, shall we?"

With a little Jelinek holding each of Mrs. Kozelle's gloved hands and another clinging to Ellie's mitten, the group threaded through a rabbit warren of rooms. Far away, Ellie heard someone wailing.

The wail grew louder as they moved deeper and deeper into the house. Finally, Jellyneck and Mrs. Kozelle shoved through a crowd at the end of a hallway. Ellie and Stan pushed after him until they were in a bedroom.

Mrs. Jelinek sat on the bed, rocking back and forth, moaning in an unearthly voice. Reverend Schuyler stood before her, an open Bible dangling from his hand, looking helpless.

"Ma!" Jellyneck screamed, throwing himself on her. "What's wrong?"

But Ellie knew. At Mrs. Jelinek's feet lay a telegram. Ellie could see the first words, "We regret to inform you . . ."

Orrie was dead.

18

Day turned to dusk. Dr. Atkinson arrived and gave Mrs. Jelinek a calming shot. Someone went down to the Do-Drop and dragged Mr. Jelinek home. More people crowded into the house.

Ellie and Stan took Jellyneck to the kitchen, the only room not jammed with drinking men and weeping women. The three friends sat at the table, staring at the scarred top. Ellie tried to think of something to say. "I'm sorry" didn't seem like enough.

"A jeep accident," Jellyneck repeated over and over. "Criminy. A jeep accident." He didn't cry. He didn't even sound as if he *might* cry. Stunned, Ellie decided. Orrie was in New Jersey. He wasn't supposed to die in a jeep accident.

The room grew darker and darker until Ellie could no longer see the water rings and nicks in the table. No one turned on the light. Somehow, the dark felt safer.

That's where Ellie's mother found them, Mrs. Kozelle at her heels.

"What are you doing sitting in the dark?" asked Mom, pulling the light chain.

"Humph," said Mrs. Kozelle, banging open cabinets, poking her head in the icebox. "Not a scrap of food in the house. Come on, Stan. We're going to get some food together. Oscar, you come too," she added.

"I wish there was coffee," Mom muttered. "Those men surely don't need any more whiskey or whatever they're drinking."

With the light on, Ellie saw the room clearly for the first time. And the baskets. Wash baskets. At least a dozen of them.

"You think the Jelineks do this much wash?" Ellie fingered a sheet. Linen, much finer than anything the McKelvey household had ever slept on. And shirts. Cotton so soft it felt like silk. Then another basket, filled with rough huck towels, some spattered with blood. *Blood?*

Then she saw the note pinned to the shirt. *Atkinson. No starch. Deliver Monday.*

Mrs. Jelinek took in laundry.

"Jeez," Ellie said. "How come we didn't know?"

"Pride," said Mom. "Taking in laundry is what the poor do."

From the front of the house, the sound of bottles breaking and a fight starting.

"Let's go," said Mom, ushering Ellie out the back door. "Things are getting out of hand."

Late that night, Ellie awoke to a faint *thump-thump-thump*. Throwing on her robe, she tiptoed to the basement.

Mom stood with her back to the stairs, running sheets through the wringer. At her feet were baskets and baskets of laundry.

Dr. Atkinson's laundry.

"It figures," sneered Victoria on Monday. "Only a Jelinek would die in a jeep accident."

"Hey, that's mean," Stan said. Still, Ellie had to admit it did seem like such an ordinary way to die.

"He won't even get a Purple Heart," mourned Stan. "If only he'd flipped that jeep in a combat zone."

For three days, Jellyneck's empty desk stuck out like a missing tooth in Room Seven. On Thursday, he came back to school.

"Nobody cares what I do anyhow," he said. Ellie fought the urge to say "So what else is new?" Jellyneck's face looked like a mask, clean in the middle, gray at the edges where the washcloth missed.

"You mean you coulda stayed home?" asked Ralph. "Are you stupid?"

Jellyneck shrugged. "Between home and here, I'd rather be here."

Miss Granberry only said, "Oscar, get your missed assignments from Stanley."

When Stan, Ellie, and Jellyneck walked home that afternoon, the hearse from Moore Brothers Funeral Parlor was parked in front of the Jelineks'. The neighbors watched from their porches as Mr. Moore and his men negotiated the casket out of the hearse and up the slippery walk and steps. Mrs. Jelinek stood in the doorway sobbing loudly, the littlest kids clinging to her skirts.

"I guess we're having the wake tonight," said Jellyneck. "If somebody can get Pa out of the Do-Drop."

He looked so forlorn that Ellie said, "We'll come to the wake, me and Stan. Won't we, Stan?" She gave Stan an elbow to the ribs.

"Oh yeah, sure," said Stan.

Jellyneck's face brightened. "Really? You'd do that?"

"Sure," said Ellie, with a casualness she didn't feel. "What're friends for?"

"Have you gone squirrelly again?" Stan asked Ellie as they slip-slid their way home. "Our folks are never gonna let us go to a wake at the Jelineks'. They'd sooner let us go to the Do-Drop."

"We're doing this for Jellyneck," Ellie pointed out.

Their mothers not only agreed to let them go to the wake, they went with them. It was last Saturday all over again, with adults and teenagers in the yard passing around bottles in bags. Ellie felt like Miss Goody Two-shoes in her Sunday dress and shoes, picking her way around men and boys in work clothes and overalls who had had too much to drink.

"Gosh, I hope we don't have to hunt all over for Jelly-neck," Stan whispered. "Those folks look rough."

They didn't have to. Jellyneck was waiting at the front door.

"Can I take your coats?" Jellyneck said, as if he were hosting a party. "Do you want to see Orrie?"

No! thought Ellie. I've never seen a dead person and I don't want to start now.

"He looks swell," Jellyneck went on. "They fixed him up good."

"Okay," said Stan. "Sure thing. Where is he?"

"This way," said Jellyneck, leading them through the crowded room, the mood somehow jovial. Like a party where the guest of honor just happened to be dead.

The open casket stood under the windows, but nobody paid Orrie any attention. People talked and laughed and drank. Only Mrs. Jelinek acted sad. She slumped on a spring-busted sofa, surrounded by women patting her hands.

"C'mon," Jellyneck urged Ellie. "Go see him. He looks good."

Someone—the Moore Brothers?—had placed torch lamps on either side of the open casket. Ellie had hoped it would be too dark to really see. Her gaze flitted around the room, stopping at the flag draped across the closed end of the casket. On to the torch lamps. Then the tattered lace curtains on the windows. Anything to avoid the open coffin, lit up like a Hollywood premiere.

Jellyneck squeezed Ellie's hand. "Just like he's sleeping, don't you think?"

Ellie gathered her courage and peered into the coffin. She stared at Orrie's hands, the nails buffed to a soft sheen, the way they never were in life, and the shiny buttons that marched up the front of his olive drab jacket.

Ellie took a deep breath, and let her gaze travel up to his face.

It wasn't Orrie.

At least not the one Ellie knew.

Even in the soft light, she could see the undertaker's heavy hand with pancake makeup, rouge, and lipstick. Ellie couldn't believe they put lipstick on a soldier. Orrie looked like a doll, with rosy cheeks and lips.

"Oh yeah," said Stan in a hearty voice. "He looks swell. Not banged up at all."

"Yeah," agreed Jellyneck.

Ellie's stomach lurched, and panic rose, like smoke from a rapidly kindling fire. She wanted to flee; she was too close to the fire.

But it wasn't Orrie who scared her.

It was Jellyneck. He was touched by death.

And death was something that Ellie did not want to get close to.

Ever.

19

So today is the first official day of spring, Ellie thought as she stomped icy snow crusts from her boots on her front porch. Ha! March 21 in Pittsburgh might just as well be January. She pulled off a mitten so she could reach into the mailbox. Bills, bills, and a letter from Jimmy!

Saturday, March 11, 1944

Dear Movie Star,

England is the berries! Strawberries, that is, in the summertime. I can't wait to taste their strawberries and cream.

Max and I have made friends with a family named Whitehurst, Mama, Papa, and two Miss Whitehursts. There's a son, too, named Clive, who is off in the Royal Air Force. One of the girls, Priscilla, is just your age. Whenever we get liberty, they invite us for supper and Mr. Whitehurst takes us to his pub, The Rose and Clover, to play darts. A pub is like the Do-Drop but without Mr. Gandeck singing to the jukebox.

Speaking of singing, have you heard "Mairzy Doats"? Some new guys brought the record with them. I hear it's a big hit in the States. I am practicing so I can embarrass you when I come back.

I spend a lot of time emptying bedpans, drawing blood and such, nothing exciting on that front. I do have a funny story, though. This general (I can't tell you who, but he's famous) was visiting the wards, handing out Purple Hearts to fellas injured in the line of duty. He asked each man how he was injured. "I was in the first wave that landed at Anzio." "I was shot in North Africa." Then the general comes to this guy who has just about every square inch of his body bandaged, both legs in traction . . . you never saw anything like it. The general says, "Soldier, where did you see action?" The soldier says, "Piccadilly Circus, sir. I got hit by a London bus on liberty, sir." It was hilarious, although I feel sorry for the fella.

Love,
Jimmy

Ellie leaned against the porch rail holding the letter, blood pounding in her ears. When she'd thought of Jimmy taking blood or emptying bedpans, she had forgotten the most important part. Patients. Wounded soldiers who had been at Anzio or North Africa. The ones that she never saw on newsreels at the Liberty, or in *Life* magazine. Those soldiers looked tired and dirty, but healthy. Not wounded.

Thank you, God, for sending Jimmy to a nice safe hospital in England.

Nobody shot guys carrying bedpans.

"Sam and Donnie want to join the service," Jellyneck said to Ellie and Stan, as the class pulled off their snow boots in the Room Seven cloakroom. "They want to take Orrie's place."

"As a jeep driver?" Ralph asked.

"Nah. They're hoping for some real frontline action. A shot at Hitler or Tojo, maybe." Jellyneck blew on his purple fingers to warm them. No gloves, Ellie noted.

"Really?" said Stan, eyes alert behind his spectacles. "What are they joining? Army? Navy? Marines?"

"But they're only high school freshmen," said Ellie.

"Sam's a freshman, Donnie's a sophomore," Jellyneck corrected. "They want Ma to sign some papers saying they're seventeen."

Ellie remembered Buddy Gandeck's friend Tennessee. "What did your mom say?" she asked.

"She said a lot of things," Jellyneck said with a twisted smile. "Mostly that she and Pa weren't signing anything, and the boys could wait until they got their draft notices when they're eighteen."

"What did they say about that?" Stan unwrapped his scarf and slung it on a coat hook.

" 'Aw, Ma, the war will be over by then.' " Jellyneck carefully draped his new jacket on the hook.

"And your Ma said . . ." Stan prompted.

" 'That's what I'm counting on.' "

Spring arrived ever so slowly in Pittsburgh. Even though the calendar said April, winter lingered on. The cinder-crusted snowdrifts dwindled, then grew tall and white again with new snow. The sidewalks were always wet, and so were Ellie's feet as her galoshes sprung bigger and bigger leaks. Ellie knew better than to ask for new rubber galoshes; there weren't any. Every night she cut new cardboard insoles for them, and every afternoon she took them out, wet and ruined. Spring couldn't come soon enough for Ellie.

"Time to put in the garden soon," Mom said, paging through the Burpee seed catalog. Ellie knew Mom wasn't going to plant in the snow. She meant it was time to plan this year's Victory Garden.

"Early Jewel, June Pink, Jubilee," Mom murmured, studying the pages at the kitchen table as Ellie cut new insoles. "Golden Queen, Marglobe."

Ellie sighed. How could such pretty names be for tomatoes? Ellie hated tomatoes with a passion. She didn't like them raw, fried, or stewed. Especially not stewed. Besides, tomato plants were a pain to take care of.

"Golden Queen it is." Mom, on the other hand, loved tomatoes. Every year the garden seemed to be two-thirds tomatoes, and a few rows of other things like snap beans and cucumbers and turnips.

Ellie looked down a long vista of hot summer days of hoeing and weeding and picking off bugs. And for what? A lot of turnips and tomatoes. It hardly seemed worth it. Maybe she could wait for spring after all. Ellie sighed, and fit the insoles into her boots.

On Macken Street, the first sign of spring was not the first robin or daffodils. The first sign of spring was Mr. Green's scoreboard. The first day of baseball season, he always hung the chalkboard with DRINK COCA-COLA across the top, just outside the store's front door.

"It's spring!" Ellie and Stan said, checking the score of the Pirates' first game of the year. Never mind that it was 42 degrees and a stiff wind shot straight through their jackets. It almost didn't matter that Pittsburgh lost to St. Louis 0–2 that first game. Win or lose, baseball meant spring.

Right after that, the school turned off the heat. Warm or not, every year the furnace stopped running on April 20. Miss Granberry opened the windows, and the cold breeze scoured away the winter smells—wet wool and Vicks VapoRub and months of Victoria's salami sandwiches.

Open windows made it harder for Ellie to concentrate. Every little sound grabbed her attention. Bicycle bells. The janitor emptying trash into the rubbish barrel. The flag flapping on the pole out front.

Ellie was trying to ignore those sounds one late April afternoon as Miss Granberry explained how to figure interest on a bank account. She might as well have been speaking Latin, for all that Ellie understood. It was the warmest day so far, and Ellie could hardly keep her eyes open, let alone listen to Miss Granberry go on and on about compound interest.

Slam! Slam! Ellie's drooping eyelids jerked open. Car doors? In front of the school? Who would drive to the school, especially so late in the day? Who drove at all, anymore? Dr. Atkinson, Reverend Schuyler, and . . .

"Holy Toledo!" Victoria shouted, leaning out the window. "It's Mr. Wheeler, and some lady."

"Sit down, Victoria," Miss Granberry said. Whatever else she said was lost in the rush of sixth graders stampeding to the windows.

Ellie peered over Stan's shoulder. Sure enough, the Western Union man's elderly Ford was at the curb. Mr. Wheeler and a woman in a housedress and apron hurried up the school steps.

Who is that lady? Ellie wondered. She was too old to be the mother of a student.

"Uh-oh," said Jellyneck. "Somebody's getting bad news."

Miss Granberry marched over to the sixth graders, all pressing for a better view. "Sit down, all of you," she rasped, shepherding the students back to their desks. "If you are going to act like first graders every time that . . ." Her voice trailed off as she looked out the window. She hastened to the hall door, then turned toward them.

"I'm leaving for a bit," she said. "Bridget will be room monitor."

And then she was gone, leaving the door open.

"Whaddya think?" Stan whispered to Ellie. "You think that telegram is for Miss Granberry?"

Ellie shook her head. "She doesn't have any relatives, I don't think."

"Stan, Ellie, I see you." Bridget noisily chalked their names on the blackboard.

"Oh, blow it out your barracks bag," Ellie said.

Bridget hastily erased the names.

Victoria sauntered over to the door and looked out.

"See anything?" Stan asked.

"Nope. No, hold on a second." Victoria motioned for the class to hush. Ellie heard the *clop click* of adult shoes on the polished floors.

"Who is it?" Bridget asked, forgetting she was in charge.

Moving back in the doorway, Victoria peeked around the doorframe. "Miss Deetch, Miss Granberry, Mr. Wheeler, and that lady, whoever she is. And they're coming this way." Victoria flung herself back into her seat.

The room sat in dead silence, waiting, waiting, for . . . for what? *Click clop click clop*. The steps came closer and closer and . . . stopped. The sound of knocking on a door. The door creaking open, then shut. Mumbled voices.

Then, the scream. The scream that sounded the same, no matter if it was a man, woman, or child.

Ellie put her head on her desk and covered her ears. *When will the war be over?*

By school the next morning, everyone on Macken Street knew that Mr. Miller, the fourth grade teacher's husband, was lost at sea. Suddenly, Mrs. Miller's students were the most popular kids in the schoolyard, as the other kids pumped them for information.

"That lady with Mr. Wheeler," a fourth-grade girl told Ellie and Stan, "was Mrs. Miller's mother. Mrs. Miller's staying with her while her husband is overseas. *Was* overseas." The girl sounded confused. "Alls I know is we got a substitute for the rest of the year."

Overnight, a gold star flag appeared on Mrs. Miller's classroom door. Ellie fought the urge to spit on the floor each time she passed it. She wished the gold star would disappear.

Incredibly, it did!

"Am I seeing things, or is that a blue star on Mrs. Miller's door?" Ellie whispered to Stan as the class marched off to assembly a few mornings later. Miss Granberry's head whipped around to see who was not being "a silent citizen in the halls," as she called it. Stan just shrugged, as if to say "Looks like it, but I don't know any more than you."

Trust Victoria to know the whole story. Of course.

"Mr. Miller isn't dead," Victoria told them at lunch. "Pa got the lowdown at the Do-Drop last night."

"So . . . ?" Stan prompted.

"So, it seems there were *two* guys named Joe Miller on the same ship," Victoria began, obviously enjoying being "in the know."

"The ship didn't sink?" Jellyneck butted in. Victoria gave him a ferocious look.

"Who's telling this story?" she said, waving a fist in his face. "So anyway, Mrs. Miller's Joe Miller got real sick before the ship left."

"Why was he sick?" Bridget interrupted.

"I don't know," Victoria said in an exasperated way. "You wanna hear this or not?"

Everyone assured her they did.

"So anyway, he's sick, and he goes to sick bay in port. 'Sick bay' is Navy for hospital," she added before anyone could ask. "Someone fouls up his paperwork, so no one knows he ain't on the ship. But the other Joe Miller is. The ship sinks and the Navy sends out telegrams that everybody's dead. Meanwhile, Mrs. Miller's husband gets well and finds out that his ship is sunk. He figures he better let his wife know he's okay. So she gets another telegram saying he's alive. Pretty incredible, hunh?"

"Yeah," Jellyneck repeated softly. "Pretty incredible."

20

No more pencils, no more books, no more teacher's dirty looks," Stan and Jellyneck chanted one May morning, fake-punching each other in rhythm.

"There's still two more weeks," Ellie reminded them. She perched on the school bike rack, enjoying the breeze on her bare knees, free at last of wool stockings. The sweater Mom insisted she wear lay in a heap on her books.

"Uh-oh," said Stan, looking toward the street. "Here comes Victoria. Something's up, I can tell."

Victoria pranced up to the trio at the bike racks, excitement fairly shooting from the ends of her hair. Instinctively, Ellie leaned away.

"Buddy's coming home," Victoria shouted. "Pa's going to San Francisco to get him."

"Thought he was in Hawaii," Jellyneck said.

"He was. The docs sent him to a veterans' hospital in

California to rest," Victoria said, sounding rather vague. "Pa's leaving as soon as he can book a compartment."

A train compartment? thought Ellie. Since when do the Gandecks have that kind of money? Compartments with berths and private bathrooms were expensive and hard to come by. Passengers counted themselves lucky to have a seat, instead of sitting on their suitcase or standing in the aisle for days at a time.

"How come?" Ellie asked. "Can't he get home by himself?"

Victoria scowled. "Because he's been *sick*, Ellie McKelvey, that's why! He needs a little help, Pa says."

"Oh." Ellie noticed Victoria clenching her fists at her sides. Not like she was going to hit somebody. Ellie herself did that when she was nervous. What did Victoria have to be nervous about?

Stan cracked his knuckles. "He's being discharged?"

Victoria looked away. "An honorable medical discharge," she said, as if daring them to say otherwise.

"When's he gonna get here? You gonna have a party when he comes home? Mr. Green gonna bring ice cream?" Jellyneck asked.

"Party, sure thing," Victoria said, her old confident self again. "It'll take Pa a week to get out there, if he's lucky. And as long coming back. Two weeks, I guess."

The first bell rang, and they scurried to their march-in lines. But Ellie continued to puzzle. Buddy wasn't wounded. Just tired. So why was he being discharged?

Those last two weeks of school seemed both long and short to Ellie. Long because the temperature zoomed into the nineties, unheard of for Pittsburgh in May. By dismissal, the boys had rolled up their sleeves and the girls had rolled down their knee socks. Ellie envied the girls whose mothers let them wear short socks before June first.

But in those fourteen sweltering days, so much else happened.

Mr. Gandeck left for San Francisco. Ellie watched him plod to the trolley stop, looking strange and uncomfortable in his Sunday suit, Victoria clutching his hand. He was on his way to Union Station to catch the *Capitol Limited* to Chicago, where he would board the *City of San Francisco*. His itinerary had been the main subject of Victoria's conversation for days.

"Bye, Mr. Gandeck," Ellie hollered, and waved. "Have a good trip."

"Thanks, girlie," he called without waving, since he had a suitcase in one hand and Victoria clinging to the other.

Clang clang. The Number 10, with Mr. Gandeck aboard, disappeared down the hill. Victoria's shoulders slumped as she turned to go, then her eyes met Ellie's. She squared her shoulders, jammed her hands in her pockets, and sauntered toward home, whistling "Mairzy Doats."

Lucky duck, thought Ellie. At least one of her brothers is coming home.

The ground had finally thawed enough to put in the Victory Garden. This year, with Mom at work and Pop's bum leg still acting up, the digging, hoeing, and planting fell mostly to Toots.

"Fine by me," she said. "Not like anybody else around here can do a fair job of it."

Ellie was grateful, because once she had weeded and watered the garden, she was free for the afternoon.

Free, that is, to do the housework, start supper, and water the increasingly crispy Christmas tree in the living room.

Decoration Day came in the middle of the last week of school. No matter what the calendar said, Decoration Day was the first day of summer, the way Labor Day was the last.

Decoration Day also meant the school picnic at West View Park. Everyone went, even people without kids. The kids ate Victory Burgers (a little hamburger mixed with a whole lot of soy extender) and ice cream and soda, and rode as many rides as they had tickets for.

Every kid got a strip of ten tickets for food and rides when they walked into the park. Ellie, Stan, and Jellyneck had worked out a scheme, taking turns coming in each of the three park entrances. It was a fine plan that would've been perfect if Jellyneck hadn't had three Victory Burgers and two Grapettes before riding the Dips four times in a row.

"Remind me not to do that at the Labor Day picnic," he said after returning from the bushes, looking green around the gills. "Here, kids." He handed the rest of his tickets to a pair of his little brothers. "Ellie, could you take them on the carousel?"

Ellie plopped the young Jelineks on a stationary carousel bench, and picked out a white horse with a gold bridle for herself. The barrel organ cranked out "My Wild Irish Rose" as the ride picked up speed. A clean, warm breeze tickled her nose. I am nothing but happy, Ellie thought.

With the doctor's bills caught up and a little extra money coming in, Mom had been able to buy Ellie a new dress for the picnic. They had gone Downtown to Kaufmann's one Saturday so Ellie could pick it out herself, a pale blue check, trimmed with red rickrack. While they were there, Ellie also got new sandals, ankle straps with *heels*. Little ones, but heels all the same because Mom said Ellie could spend her shoe ration coupon any way she wanted.

Ellie had pinned up her braids in a more grownup style for the occasion. Without Sal around, Ellie felt . . . well . . . *pretty*. Not like a saddle-shoe smudge at all.

After the carousel ride, Ellie delivered the boys back to Jellyneck and Stan, who took them off to try their luck at the shooting gallery. Feeling far too mature to shoot at tin ducks with a popgun, Ellie sauntered along the shady cinder path that circled the park.

I'll be twelve in July, Ellie thought. Practically a teenager. A bobby-soxer. She tried out Sal's hip-rolling stroll. She was sure she looked at least fourteen, and maybe even a little hubba-hubba. She wondered if she should have worn Jimmy's stockings.

"Mairzy doats and dozy doats and liddle lamzy divy," Ellie hummed over and over. She could never remember the rest of the words. She was trying to think of them when her sandal heel caught on something, and she sprawled face down in the cinders.

That's what you get for thinking you're such hot stuff, she scolded herself.

"Beg pardon, miss," said a man's voice. "Are you hurt?"

"No," said Ellie, feeling foolish. She looked up to see that the voice belonged to a soldier. On crutches. A soldier with one leg. His empty trouser leg was neatly pinned out of the way.

"I'd give you a hand, except I don't have one to spare," he joked. "But I do apologize. I'm still getting used to these darn things." He jerked his head toward the crutches. "I'm always tripping folks."

Ellie got to her feet, brushing cinders from the skirt of her dress. "No, it's my fault. I'm so clumsy."

"Join the club, sister," he said with a laugh. But not like he thought it was funny.

The soldier went on his way, good leg swinging between the wooden supports. Ellie realized he was the first soldier she had ever seen who wasn't just fine. Soldiers in movies either died or came back with a trunkful of medals.

Nobody came back with one leg.

Two days later, Miss Granberry handed out the last report cards, and school was over for the year. For the sixth grade, it was their last day at Macken Street Grammar School.

No dismissal lines today. Most of the class shot out the door without a backward glance. Ellie and Stan took the time to say goodbye to their teacher.

"Don't forget to come back for a visit," Miss Granberry said, packing her teaching supplies in a Fels-Naptha soap box.

"Yes, Miss Granberry." Ellie's eyes strayed to the Honor Wall. When had it grown so large, covering the wall from corner to corner? So many gold stars. "Are you taking down the pictures?"

"No, dear," said Miss Granberry. "They will stay until the war is over." She gave a tiny sigh, then went back to loading books in the Fels-Naptha box.

Ellie bid a silent farewell to Sean and Otis and Sy and the rest. *Don't worry, fellas. We'll beat that Hitler and the Japs, too. You'll see.*

Too bad Jimmy never sent that snapshot to Ellie for the Honor Wall. In a way, she was glad he hadn't. Without him up there, she wasn't reminded he was gone every time she sharpened her pencil.

"This is the last time," Ellie said to Stan as they started down the staircase. "We'll never come back." Her hand trailed along the sun-warmed banister and she wished she'd slid down it, like Jimmy.

At home, a thick Jimmy letter waited in the mailbox for Ellie. Though she was dying to put on shorts and sneakers and officially start summer vacation, Ellie decided the letter came first.

She ripped into the envelope, contents spilling to the porch. Sinking to the cool cement floor, she gathered the scattered bits into her lap. One sheet of paper? Did Jimmy forget the rest of the letter? No. "Your loving brother, Jimmy" was at the bottom. The rest of the bulk was photographs of people Ellie didn't recognize.

Saturday, April 29, 1944

Dear Movie Star,

Here are the snapshots I've been meaning to send. I've been pretty busy, so it took a while to get these developed at the PX. One is of me and Max, all spiffed up for a night on the town. Handsome dudes, don't you think?

Ellie shuffled through the photos until she came to one of two soldiers in front of a building labeled BARRACKS D. A short fellow, curly hair creeping from beneath his overseas cap. His companion a sharp-jawed, hard-eyed young man with a familiar grin. She *knew* it was Jimmy, but he looked so much older, almost like a stranger. A hollow space opened in her heart, as if Jimmy had left a second time. Turning the picture over, she read, in a penciled scribble, *This one is for Miss G.*

Suddenly, it was last September and she was telling Jimmy about Miss Granberry's wall. Looking back, that now seemed like the happiest day of her life. Ellie gulped away the lump in her throat as she returned to the letter.

Another is of the Whitehursts, the family I told you about. That's Mum and Da and their daughters, Eileen and Priscilla. The dog is named Betts, after Princess Elizabeth.

The Whitehursts posed stiffly before a mantel cluttered with empty vases and dog figurines. A plumpish mother in a lace-collared dress and sensible shoes sat upright in an armchair, ankles crossed in a ladylike way. Next to her, the father, with sunken cheeks but merry-looking eyes, a spaniel asleep on his shoes. Dentures, Ellie decided. His cheeks caved in like Grampa Guilfoyle's.

Beside the adults stood two girls. One looked a bit younger than Sal, with rimless spectacles, frowsy hair, and a too-big cardigan. Sal would've called her a drip.

Next to the Drip, a chunky girl, with stubby braids, leaned against her mother's chair. Her stockings wrinkled at the ankles, cardigan gaping between the buttons. She clutched a framed picture to her chest.

Cilla is holding a picture of her brother, Clive. He's in the Royal Air Force but they wanted him in the family picture. They send their regards, and hope that after the war, we can all get together. Wouldn't that be something?

A red mist rose before Ellie's eyes.
She shook her head to clear it, and flipped through the

rest of the snapshots. Jimmy and Max. In a jeep. Toasting a pair of Army nurses with Coca-Colas. Marching.

The last was of Jimmy and Priscilla, her shoulders hunched under the weight of an accordion, frowning down at the keys. Jimmy's head was thrown back, mouth wide open, obviously singing along.

When I get homesick for the Gandecks, Cilla plays "Oh Marie" on her squeezebox. She knows "The Hut-Sut Song," too. I am teaching her "Mairzy Doats." She's some musician.

I go on duty soon, so I'll sign off now. Please give that picture to Miss Granberry for me.

Your loving brother,
Jimmy, The Singing Sensation of the U.S. Army

Ellie crammed the pictures and letter back into the envelope. No fair that this Cilla girl could joke and sing with Jimmy and she, Ellie, couldn't. She let herself into the house, banging the door behind her.

"Hey!" Toots shouted from upstairs. "There's a lady up here trying to sleep."

"Sorry," Ellie yelled back as she stomped to her room. But she wasn't sorry she'd woken up Toots. She was sorry the world wasn't fair.

No fair that Victoria's brother got a Hawaiian vacation, and then could come home. No fair that Toots lived in

Jimmy's room. No fair that Sal got paid at Green's for mixing a few sodas and flirting with boys. Ellie wanted to get even with the whole world, but she couldn't think how. But she knew where she could start.

She yanked open her underwear drawer and buried the envelope beneath her slips and underpants. *You can just stay there, Jimmy-the-Promise-Breaker. You didn't come home for Christmas. You didn't tell me you were going to England. And now you're singing "The Hut-Sut Song" with some accordion-playing English girl. No fair!*

Arky Vaughan gave Ellie a reproachful look from his home inside the mirror frame. *Promise breaker,* he seemed to say. *You told Jimmy you'd put his picture on Miss Granberry's wall.*

I don't have to keep my promise, she told Arky. *Jimmy didn't keep his promise, so I'm not keeping mine. Besides, school's over.*

Slamming the drawer, Ellie went downstairs to water the Christmas tree.

After all, it wasn't the tree's fault that Jimmy welshed on a deal.

21

Ellie sucked the last of the strawberry ice cream from the bottom of her cone.

"June 6, 1944, D-Day," she said, savoring the date as much as the ice cream. "We'll remember it our whole lives. The Allies invade Europe."

Swiveling her counter stool around to face the room, Ellie surveyed the mob scene in Green's. The store was packed with adults and kids in a holiday mood. And not just because Mr. Green had scrawled across his scoreboard, *Forget the Pirates! The Yanks have landed in France! Free ice cream as long as it lasts!*

"Yeah," said Victoria, agreeable, for once. "We can tell our kids about D-Day and how the Americans kicked Hitler's butt." She spun her chair around and around until she was just a blur to Ellie.

"They haven't kicked it yet," Stan reminded her.

"But they're gonna." Jellyneck dreamily licked at the chocolate that ringed his mouth.

"Yeah," said Bridget. "My da says it's the beginning of the end of the war."

"If you kids are finished, scram," Sal yelled from behind the counter. "We need the seats." Sal's hair drooped from the ponytail she wore to work, her face beet-red as she scooped cone after cone. Mr. Green was scooping too, but mostly he schmoozed with the customers.

"Yes, that's my Ruthie," he said, waving a dripping scooper at her service portrait over the cash register. "She's in Washington, D.C., helping beat them Nazis, you betcha."

"I mean, make like a tree and leave. Now!" said Sal, viciously attacking a tub of chocolate ice cream.

"All right, all right, keep your shirt on," said Ellie, taking as much time as she dared, slowly sliding from the stool and sauntering out the door with the rest of the gang.

Outside, they stood on the sidewalk looking at each other. The Number 10 rattled past, people hanging out the windows, banging on the sides of the car, cheering. "Hooray for Ike!" "Hooray for General Eisenhower!" "Hitler is a dead man!"

"Yeah, good old Ike," came a slurry shout from the Do-Drop.

The evening sky was still light, thanks to War Time. Supper was hours ago. No one wanted to go home. The end of the war was just around the corner. What other miracles could the day hold?

Ralph Stankavitch, who at long last had passed to junior high, swaggered down the block, hands in his shorts pockets. As he came closer, Ellie heard him singing to the tune of "Whistle While You Work":

Whistle while you work
Hitler is a jerk
Mussolini bit his weenie
Now it doesn't work.

Their parents and teachers had asked them a million times to *please* not sing that song. But today was special. The song belonged to today. All bets were off today. General Ike and the Yanks were winning the war and anything could happen today.

"Anybody want to play Commando Kelly?" Victoria asked.

Commando Kelly was big news that spring. He was from the North Side, too, only a couple trolley stops away. Ellie wasn't clear on all the details, but one thing was certain: he was Pittsburgh's first Medal of Honor winner.

Ellie didn't like playing war, but she didn't want to go home, either.

"Sure," she said, along with everyone else.

"Okay, ante up for the 7-Up," Victoria ordered. Hands dug through pockets for enough pennies. You couldn't play Commando Kelly without a bottle of 7-Up.

"Meet at the park picnic shelter at twenty-hundred

hours." When Victoria played Commando Kelly, she played it all the way, right down to using military time.

The kids arrived at the park shelter as the St. Matthew's bell tolled eight. Although Ellie had found a rifle-sized tree branch on the way, she knew that she would wind up being a nurse or a peasant or something else unimportant. Victoria was *always* Commando Kelly.

The first lightning bugs blinked in the shadows as Victoria gathered her troops, assigning roles. To Ellie's surprise, Victoria picked her for Commando Kelly's platoon.

"It's the Battle of Salerno," Victoria began. "The Americans have landed on the Italian coast. Brave Commando Kelly crawls two miles under enemy fire to spy on enemy positions."

That was Stan and Jellyneck's cue as German soldiers to open fire.

"Ba-room!" shouted Stan, aiming his bazooka, a battered two-by-four.

"Eh-eh-eh-eh," Jellyneck stuttered in his best machine gun imitation, aiming his old drill rifle at Victoria as she crawled through the grass. Ellie inhaled the damp night smell and waited for her orders from Commando Victoria.

"And back," Victoria announced. She reversed herself, still under Stan and Jellyneck's barrage of fire.

"Okay, men." Commando Kelly waved to the rest of her group—Ellie and Ralph. "Follow me."

Commando Kelly and her platoon killed seventy Germans before they reached the picnic shelter. Ellie knew this because they counted. "Forty-one, another Kraut dead. Forty-two, another Kraut dead," Victoria shouted as Stan and Jellyneck took turns falling down dead.

At last, the Americans secured the picnic shelter.

"Men, a safe place to hide from the enemy," Victoria announced. "The house of a peasant."

On cue, Bridget welcomed Commando Victoria. *"Signore Americano,"* she said in a terrible Italian accent. "Pleeze welcome to me humble home." She thumped the open bottle of 7-Up on the picnic table. *"Mama mia,"* she added for no good reason.

Victoria peered from an imaginary window. "I spy a nest of Nazi snipers," she announced. She shouldered her broken air rifle and opened fire on the Nazis. Stan and Jellyneck pretended to die again.

"I wish we had a couple more kids," Stan said. "All I do is die over and over."

"Shut up!" yelled Victoria. "Yunz supposed to be dead." She reached for the 7-Up.

"Why, look, a bottle of champagne. I ain't never drunk champagne. I think I'll try some while I'm shooting Krauts." Victoria fired with one hand while swigging the pop with the other. "Why, this champagne ain't so much. It tastes just like 7-Up." The real Commando Kelly had found champagne in his cottage hideout, and had said that it tasted like 7-Up.

"It *is* 7-Up," Ellie said.

Victoria slammed down her 7-Up champagne. "What did you say?"

"Take it back," shouted Stan, rising from the dead again.

But it was too late. The next thing Ellie knew, Germans, Americans, and Italians were punching each other, rolling in the tall park grass. Ellie found herself flat on her back, Victoria sitting on her stomach.

"Say uncle," Victoria hollered, twisting Ellie's arm. Then, without warning, she let go and took off toward the street.

"Hey, Commando Kelly," Ralph hollered. "Where yunz going?"

"Taxi, going up the hill," she called back. "Maybe it's Pa and Buddy."

The rest of the troops abandoned battle and scrambled toward the street after Victoria. Once on the pavement, they broke into a full run, following the taxicab up Macken Street.

Block after block, the cab toiled up the hill, the kids pounding right behind.

"I think it *is* Buddy," Victoria puffed. "See the Marine hat in the back window?"

The taxi braked in front of the Gandecks', shuddering to a halt. Victoria stopped short, the rest of the gang piling into her. Ellie held her breath as the rear door opened. Mr. Gandeck's big behind backed out on the street side. He stood, rumpled and blinking, staring into the backseat.

"Where's Buddy?" Victoria launched herself into her father's arms, looking expectantly at the cab, where no one was getting out.

Gently, Mr. Gandeck disentangled himself from Victoria. He motioned to the cab driver, who walked around to the open door.

"Son," Mr. Gandeck called softly. "We're home, son."

"Home?" a quavery voice answered.

"That's right, pal," said the cab driver in a gentle voice. "Lemme give you a hand."

The cabbie and Mr. Gandeck leaned into the car, and pulled out a scarecrow of a man, in a sizes-too-big Marine uniform. The cabbie slung the soldier's arm around Mr. Gandeck's neck. There he hung, like so much wet laundry.

Oh my gosh, thought Ellie. Mr. Gandeck brought home the wrong soldier.

This soldier was skinny and hollow-eyed, skin the color of a Halloween pumpkin.

"Buddy?" Victoria stood stock-still on the sidewalk.

The soldier's eyes flickered. "Hey, Lil Sis," he said in a flat voice. "How's tricks?"

"Why is he orange?" whispered Jellyneck. "Is that jungle rot?"

"Naw," said Ralph in not-quite-a-whisper. "It's some kind of medicine they give soldiers to keep them from getting malaria. Turns their skin that color."

The cabbie plunked a valise and a duffel bag on the sidewalk. Ellie, Stan, Jellyneck, and the rest of the gang just stood there, not knowing what to do.

The cabdriver cleared his throat. "Um . . . mister, about the fare . . ."

Mr. Gandeck blinked, as if coming out of a trance. "I'm

sorry," he said, reaching inside his jacket, with Buddy still clinging to his neck.

"Too bad he come home so late today," Jellyneck stage-whispered. "Mr. Green already give away all his ice cream. No party tonight."

Mr. Gandeck paid the cab fare, then turned to Jellyneck.

"You're right, sonny," Mr. Gandeck said in a sad voice. "No party tonight."

22

ut it's my birthday, Mom," Ellie wailed. "Tuesday? July 25? Did you forget? Please don't make me do the dumb old canning today."

Mom set a sealed Mason jar of stewed tomatoes on the drainboard, then went to the sink to wash tomato goo from her hands. The back screen door banged open, and Aunt Toots, still in her work overalls, lugged in still another bushel basket of tomatoes. Ellie shuddered with disgust.

"I'm sorry, but you had a day off when you went to North Park with Stan last week." Mom swiped peanut butter across two slices of bread, slapped them together, and wrapped the sandwich in wax paper. "We have tomatoes coming out of our ears. Be a shame to let them rot on the vine." She dropped the sandwich in her lunch bucket and snapped it shut. "Besides, you only have to can until Sal goes to work."

It was Toots's day off from work. Maybe she could do the canning. Ellie shot her a look, but Toots said "Don't even ask" before Ellie could open her mouth. "I did my bit yesterday morning. Just brought these in now"—Toots heaved the basket to the countertop—"to save you and Sal the trouble." She dusted her hands on the seat of her overalls. "I'm going to catch a few winks and meet the girls at West View Park." Toots gave Ellie a nudge in passing. "No sense wasting a day off sleeping."

Or canning tomatoes, Ellie thought as she glared at the pots bubbling on the stove. One contained Mason jars and lids, sterilizing. The other, disgusting, burbling tomatoes. She swished the mixture with a wooden spoon. Hot juice burped over the edge, spattering Ellie's bare elbow.

"Ouch!" she hollered. Upstairs, the shower sputtered to life and Mom shouted, "Rise and shine, Sally Jane. There's a bushel of tomatoes with your name on it."

"I'm twelve today," Ellie told the stove. "And I have to spend it with you." She kicked the corner of the stove. The stove didn't notice, but Ellie's toes did. "Stupid old stove," she muttered.

Mom breezed back through, grabbing her lunch bucket from the drain board. "Bye, sweetheart. I know this isn't much of a birthday but . . ."

"It's only for the duration," Ellie finished for her.

Mom hugged Ellie. "Happy birthday, my baby." And she was gone.

Ellie had had her birthday all planned. Strawberry pancakes for breakfast. A swim at North Park. A nice long session with *Gone with the Wind*, which she had snitched from Sal. Chocolate cake at supper, with everyone singing "Happy Birthday." That's what she had planned.

Instead, Ellie and Sal spent the morning peeling and chopping tomatoes. The tomatoes hissed and spit back at them.

"Looks like someone got murdered in here," Ellie said, smacking tomato seeds from her hands. Pulp and juice dripped from cabinet doors, splattered across the linoleum.

"Kind of looks like rubies," said Sal, admiring a finished jar. "Pretty, hunh?"

"If you like tomatoes," Ellie grunted. Judging from what was left in the bushel baskets and the garden, she figured they had enough to feed General Patton's army. The Russian army, too.

And this was only the beginning. Soon, there would be cucumbers to pickle. And beans . . . Snap, string, butter. Ellie had never taken much notice of canning, since Mom had done it all herself. Well, she noticed now!

After a very long morning, a row of gleaming red jars lined the kitchen countertop. "I don't want to touch another tomato. Ever," Sal said. "The first jar was pretty, but after five or six . . ." She wiped her hands, leaving red smears on the dishtowel.

"And how," Ellie agreed, picking a tomato peel out of her hair.

"I'm going to get ready for work." Sal flew out of the kitchen, leaving Ellie to clean up.

She was still mopping up the canning debris when Sal bounced back downstairs. In her mint-green dress and jaunty ponytail, she didn't look like she had been hovering over a stewpot all morning. I feel like a sweaty mess, Ellie gloomed. Probably look like one, too.

"Why so glum, little chum?" Sal chucked Ellie under the chin. "Come over to the store later, and I'll make you a sundae for your birthday. On the house."

"Okay," said Ellie as Sal skipped off, ponytail swinging. It wasn't a birthday cake, but it was better than nothing.

Ellie fixed herself a peanut butter sandwich and took it out on the back stoop. It wasn't any cooler, but at least she was out of the kitchen. The tomato smell left a tinny taste in her mouth. Like blood, she thought, remembering the day last fall when Victoria had socked her in the mouth.

Funny, she hadn't seen much of Victoria since Buddy had come home. She saw her in Corsiglia's market sometimes, or sitting on the porch with Buddy. But she never spoke, so neither did Ellie.

Twirl-twirl. Twirl-twirl. Ellie raced through the house to answer the door, arriving in time to catch Mr. Carlson at the top of the terrace.

"Hey there, Ellie," he called. "Think you've got mail from Jimmy."

"Thanks," she called. Her heart jumped when she pulled

out an envelope with her name scrawled in Jimmy's writing.

> Twinkle, twinkle, Movie Star,
> How I wonder how you are.
> Wish I may and wish I might
> Have a slice of your cake tonight.

OK, I'm no Emily Dickinson. Happy birthday, Movie Star. Big doings over here in England, but I'll tell you about that later. I'll be thinking about you on your special day.

Ellie tucked the envelope in her shorts pocket with a loving pat. The weight of the letter reminded her of Jimmy as she plowed through the afternoon chores. Dusting. Vacuuming. The half-cleaned kitchen still awaited her, but somehow Ellie couldn't make herself go back in there.

Later, she told herself. I'll clean up before I start supper.

The kitchen clock said it was three o'clock. Hours before anyone would be home. Should she go over to Green's for her sundae? Or wait until after supper? She'd rather read on the porch now and save the sundae for after supper. It would be something to look forward to.

It was one of those breathless, gray-sky days when the smoke from the steel mills drifted toward North Side. Stretching out on the glider, Ellie kicked off her tomato-spattered sneakers and wiggled her hot toes on the cool cement floor. *Squeak screech* sang the glider as she pushed herself back and forth.

Gray skies, hot kitchens, and the aroma of *eau de tomato* faded as Ellie fell headfirst into *Gone with the Wind*. Scarlett O'Hara and the swaying glider took her far away from Macken Street. So far away, she didn't hear the footsteps on the terrace walk. Or on the porch.

Twirl-twirl. Twirl-twirl.

Fred, the Western Union boy, stood at the door, poised to give the bell another twist. Ellie sat up.

"Sorry. Didn't see you." Fred flushed, whether from heat or embarrassment, Ellie couldn't tell. "Is your mother home?"

"She's at work," Ellie said briefly. She didn't want to waste time talking to Fred. Scarlett O'Hara had just killed a Yankee soldier!

"How about Sal?" Fred's voiced squeaked.

"She's working. At Green's," Ellie said, expecting him to fly off the porch in the direction of the candy store.

Fred didn't move.

"Are you lost or something? I thought Western Union didn't get lost."

"Is anyone home besides you?" Fred's voice squeaked like the glider.

"No," said Ellie. "Everybody's at work or something."

Fred gulped once. Twice. *What's the matter with him?*

Then she saw the telegram.

23

Slap slap slap. Someone was smacking her hand. Smell of vanilla and butterscotch. Ellie opened her eyes. Philco radio. Green bridge lamp. Rose chintz rocker. Stan's house. *How did I get here?*

"Ellie?" Sal bent close, red-gold hair swinging forward, a curtain to hide them.

"Sal?" she whispered. "Fred . . ."

"I know," said Sal. "I know."

Ellie closed her eyes. She could hear someone dialing a phone. Mrs. Kozelle. "Yes . . . only one at home . . . poor thing . . . Where is her aunt?"

At West View. But it was too much effort to say so. Everything was too much effort. The whirring fan faded away in a hissing fog.

Ellie huddled in the McKelvey's phone nook, head to knees. People came and went. Lots of them. Mom was in the kitchen, crying. No one knew where Pop was.

Ellie couldn't remember how she'd gotten home.

"Ellie?"

Stan's specs reflected the hall light, blanking out the lenses.

"You want some food?" He held out a plate. "There's lots of good stuff. Ham and cake and pierogies."

Pierogies. They'd had pierogies at Jimmy's going-away party.

"No, thanks, Stan."

Creak slam bang. Over and over. *Creak slam bang.* Now Ellie knew why Mom hated a banging screen door.

So many people. Mr. Corsiglia in his grocer's apron. Trudy, her face as white as her butcher's coat. Mrs. Kozelle, directing the action like a traffic cop. "Put that soda pop on the porch. Bring that cake over here. No, don't bother Mrs. McKelvey."

Reverend Schuyler and his Bible. His lips moved but Ellie couldn't hear him. Was he praying?

Creak slam bang.

Time passed; minutes or hours? Ellie couldn't tell. Toots and the Bettys arrived, clutching West View souvenirs, Stan right behind them. He must have gone to the park to get them. How did he find them?

The Bettys rolled up their sleeves and went into action. Cleaning the kitchen mess Ellie had forgotten. The red-headed Betty went with Sal to look for Pop. Someone must have put water on to boil, because soon Ellie heard the teakettle whistle.

"Sorry, but I need the phone." Toots squeezed Ellie's shoulder. Mom's worn leather address book dangled from her hand.

Ellie moved to the hall stairs as Toots badgered the long distance operator. Once the operator connected Toots, Ellie knew from experience that her aunt would do a lot of hollering. The phone lines between Pittsburgh and Lost Gap were terrible. Lots of hissing and crackling.

"D-Day!" Toots shouted as if she were talking to West Virginia without the phone. "I said, *D-DAY, JUNE 6. THE INVASION.*"

How silly. D-Day was weeks ago.

"We just got the telegram today. There was some kind of holdup notifying families." Toots listened to the person on the other end.

"The memorial service is next Saturday. No, not a *sad day.*" Pause. "Well, yes, it is a sad day. But I said the service is *Saturday.*"

Victoria plopped down on the stairs next to Ellie.

"Sorry about your brother," Victoria said, voice low and rough. "He was a good guy."

"Yes," said Ellie. "He'll be coming home soon."

Victoria wrinkled her brow. "But they don't send bodies back from France. They bury them there."

"Jimmy's not in France." Ellie stared at Victoria. "He's a medic in England. His patients call him Doc."

Victoria cracked her knuckles, one by one. Then, in a soft voice, she said, "Sure, Ellie."

Ellie pulled the letter from her shorts pocket and waved it in Victoria's face. "See, I got this letter today. For my birthday. He's in England."

"Okay." Victoria stood, eyes not quite meeting Ellie's. "Take it easy." She disappeared into the crowded dining room.

Ellie stared at her tomato-splattered sneakers.

Creak slam bang. Dr. Atkinson elbowed his way through the living room to the kitchen. Ellie trailed behind him to see why he was at her house.

Mom sat at the kitchen table with Toots, teapot on the table, a cup of steaming tea before her. She stared past Dr. Atkinson, dry-eyed, blank-faced.

"Mrs. McKelvey, I am so sorry," said Dr. Atkinson in his soothing voice. The one he used when someone was very sick.

He put his satchel on the high stool. When he turned around, he held a hypodermic needle. The sight of the needle seemed to jolt Mom from her trance.

"What are you going to do with that?" she asked.

"I thought you needed something to ease the pain," said the doctor.

"I don't need anything, thank you," said Mom in a flat voice. "There's nothing you can do for me, doctor. There's nothing anyone can do."

"Drink your tea, Sis," Toots told Mom as Dr. Atkinson silently repacked his bag.

Sal and the redheaded Betty returned, without Pop.

"Nobody knows where he is," Sal reported to Toots between phone calls. "We went to the post office, and they said he punched out regular time. Nobody had called him there, so I guess he doesn't know."

"Unless he ran into one of the neighbors. Or worse, that numbskulled Western Union boy." Toots sighed. "He'll come home sooner or later. Just wish it were sooner."

Pop, thought Ellie. When Pop gets here, he'll straighten all this out.

Twilight filled the house, but no one turned on the lights. People left. Sal and her girlfriends were in Ellie and Sal's room with the door closed. Ellie curled up on the phone bench. Even though it was hot outside, she felt cold. So cold. Ellie hugged herself tighter.

Toots and a Betty were talking in the living room.

"We should take down the Christmas tree," said the Betty. "With all these people smoking in there, it's liable to go up like a torch."

"No!" Ellie screamed. "Not until Jimmy comes home."

Toots appeared in the hallway and knelt beside her. "Jimmy's not coming home, kiddo," she said, taking Ellie's hand. "The telegram said so."

"Oh, *that*." Ellie smiled. "They thought Mr. Miller was

dead, too. But he's fine and Mrs. Miller is fine and everyone is fine and we'll be fine too as soon as we get the other telegram. The one that says it's all a mistake."

The expression on Toots's face told Ellie that she didn't understand. That was okay. She'd explain to Toots later . . . when she could think better.

"Anybody home?" a man shouted through the screen door. In the dim porch light stood Mr. Gandeck, holding up Pop. At least Ellie thought it was Pop. He wore Pop's postal uniform, but his face was the color of ashes, wet strings of hair plastered to his forehead. When she opened the door, Ellie smelled beer.

"I'm sorry," said Mr. Gandeck as he steered Pop inside. "Some nincompoop told him the news when he got off the streetcar, then dragged him into the Do-Drop to drown his sorrows."

Speechless, Ellie stared at Pop propped against Mr. Gandeck's barrel chest. This all had to be a terrible, terrible mistake. The telegram. The swarms of neighbors. Pop drunk.

Ellie found enough voice to say, "But Pop doesn't drink. Not ever."

"I know," Mr. Gandeck said, in a sad, gentle voice. "I tried to bring him home sooner, but he wouldn't let me. I had to wait for all the fight to go out of him before I did."

Mom and Toots appeared out of the gloom. Without a

word, they guided Pop upstairs, leaving Ellie and Mr. Gandeck.

"I'm so sorry," Mr. Gandeck said, shifting his bulk from one foot to the other. "Believe you me, I know what you folks are going through, losing a son."

Ellie looked into Mr. Gandeck's blue eyes, so small in his large, beefy face. He doesn't look crazy, she thought. Maybe he's just drunk. Because we haven't lost a son, and neither has he. His son is at home right this minute. And Jimmy? He's at that hospital in England, emptying bedpans.

"Good night, Mr. Gandeck," she said, holding the screen door for him.

"Good night, girlie," he said, disappearing into the dark.

Ellie heard Pop's feet thumping on the stairs as Mom and Toots dragged him to the bedroom. *Clunk clunk.* Shoes dropping. *Sca-reech.* Bedsprings.

"As if Sis doesn't have enough trouble," Toots said in her hog-calling voice. "Straighten up, be a man."

Ellie knew Toots was talking to Pop. But nobody talked to Pop that way—not even a bigmouth like Toots.

She fled to the back stoop. *No stars tonight, Jimmy. Too cloudy.* Across the alley, she watched Mr. Gandeck trudge up his porch steps. She waited.

Mrs. Gandeck didn't yell. Mr. Gandeck didn't play "Oh Marie."

Pop's drunk, the Gandecks aren't fighting, and Victoria is acting nice. Things are all screwy. Why?

Her thoughts winked out as quickly as the Gandecks' lights.

Long after everyone had stumbled off to bed, if not to sleep, Ellie crept downstairs. She fumbled her way to the kitchen, not turning on the lights. The lingering smell of too much food surrounded her in the warm dark like an unwanted blanket. Only the linoleum felt cool to her bare feet. Opening the cupboard, she felt around for a water glass and quietly filled it. Just as quietly, she padded into the living room.

Kneeling, she poured the water in the Christmas tree stand. Dead pine needles pierced the knees of her pajamas. In the pocket of her pajama top, she felt the crinkly weight of Jimmy's letter over her heart.

He'll come home. *He promised.*

Ellie just had to wait for the Army to fix their mistake.

24

Hot, bleached-sky days followed damp, moonless nights. One day seemed like another to Ellie. The phone ringing off the hook. The house crammed with food and people. The screen door. *Bang. Slam. Bang. Slam.*

Relatives arrived by the cabload from the train station, slept in odd corners, talked in whispers. Gramma and Grampa shuffled from room to room like ghosts. Had they shrunk since Ellie had last seen them? They looked so tiny. If it weren't for Grampa's pipe and Gramma's sack of pecans, Ellie wouldn't have known them at all.

Gramma and Grampa moved into the girls' room, and Ellie and Sal moved to pallets on the porch. Night after night, Ellie listened to the adults in the yard, smoking, talking about old times, better times, before-the-war times, cicadas shrilling in the background.

Night after night, Ellie counted as St. Matthew's clock

chimed ten, eleven, twelve. The Number 10 racketed by on its last run of the night. Next to Ellie, Sal snored softly, making little hiccuping sounds. The adults were in bed, the cicadas asleep, when the bell struck one.

But Ellie was still awake.

Saturday morning, Ellie woke to voices in the yard. Beneath the window, Victoria was picking the McKelveys' tomatoes.

Who was that with her? Stan? And Jellyneck and Bridget and even Ralph, dragging bushel baskets between the rows of staked plants.

Ellie ran downstairs. Mom and Toots sat at the kitchen table, staring into teacups.

"Mom, half the neighborhood is in our garden stealing tomatoes." said Ellie. "You want me to run them off?"

"No," said Mom, turning the teacup around in her hands. "I told the neighbors to help themselves. We won't be canning anymore this summer. It's a shame to let them go to waste."

Ellie watched her friends and wished it were last week, when her worst trouble was canning tomatoes.

That telegram had to come soon, now, this morning. Before the memorial service.

Ellie thought it was strange to be in church on a Saturday morning. But even on a Saturday, church smelled like church . . . candle wax and dusty hymnbooks. And flowers.

Besides the carnations and lilies on the altar, Sal had used a heavy hand with her April Showers talc. Toots reeked of Evening in Paris, while Gramma waved a hanky scented with Lily of the Valley cologne. Wedged between Gramma and Sal, Ellie felt she might smother under all the flowery smells.

Sal elbowed Ellie in the ribs. "Quit squirming," she whispered. "Behave yourself."

Something fluttered in Ellie's heart. Not a good, expectant flutter. It felt sharp and evil, like excitement gone wrong.

Jimmy's service portrait stood on a table in front of the altar, surrounded by flowers. A steady stream of dressed-up people filled the pews. A lot of people. Almost as many as Christmas Eve. Stan and his mother, with Jellyneck in Stan's hand-me-downs. All the Gandecks, even Buddy, uniform baggy on his thin frame, chest gleaming with medals. Mr. Green in a suit, shiny with wear. The whole Corsiglia family, who weren't supposed to go anywhere but their Catholic church. Trudy, solemn and pale in a black dress, with her parents. The Bettys, in their overalls and bandannas, and Wally, fresh off the night shift.

There's a bunch of people, here, Jimmy. I don't know half of them.

Who was the kid in short pants, holding the hand of an old woman? How did Jimmy know him? Or the young man with leg braces and crutches, moving stiffly down the aisle? What about the skinny, teenaged colored girl, dressed to the nines, hesitating at the back of the church? Jimmy knew colored people?

No! Not knew! *How does he* know?

Because Jimmy isn't dead.

The evil fluttery thing stabbed Ellie's chest again. *Maybe . . . just maybe . . . Jimmy really* is *dead.*

Pain. Sharper. Like a knife in her ribs.

Okay, God. Listen. I promise I'll be good from now on if Jimmy is safe.

Again, the flutter. Stronger.

Not enough. I have to promise something big. Like not hating Victoria's guts.

But knowing that two rows back Victoria sat with her own brother, Ellie didn't think she could manage to not hate her. She'd have to think of something else.

A loud sob burped from someone. Toots? Toots looked completely unlike herself in Mom's navy dress and an old-lady hat borrowed from Gramma.

That's it. If you keep Jimmy safe, God, I'll never snoop in Toots's room again. I'll even try to like her.

Ellie waited for her heart to tell her something. She decided to thank God in advance, even though her heart wasn't sending any signals. *Thanks, God. I knew you'd keep him safe.* She smiled, and bowed her head, pretending to pray. *Hey, Jimmy, look. I'm wearing your Christmas present. Mom said this was a special occasion. Joke's on them, hunh?*

She brushed the front of her dress. Only *she* knew

Jimmy's letter was tucked inside her slip. Limp from days of handling, the letter no longer crinkled.

The organist noodled around with some music that sounded like finger exercises while the mourners filed in. When Reverend Schuyler appeared at the altar, the organist pulled out all the stops for the first hymn, "Joyful, Joyful, We Adore Thee."

After a prayer so long Ellie grew woozy, Reverend Schuyler motioned them to sit. The minister mounted the pulpit, gripped its sides, and looked out at the congregation with a mournful expression.

"We are here to remember James Armstrong McKelvey, who died in service to his country."

Ellie fiddled with her dress sash, surfacing every so often to see if the Reverend was still talking.

". . . and in my Father's house there are many mansions. If it were not so . . ."

Still talking. Ellie tuned him out.

". . . for while we are sorrowful today, a bright day will dawn when we shall see dear James again in Heaven."

After about a million years, the minister led another prayer, another hymn, and it was over. Reverend Schuyler came down from the altar to comfort the family.

Get lost, Ellie thought as the Reverend pressed a clammy hand on her head. She wanted out of church, now. Too many people, too many sickly-sweet flower smells, and, most important, Fred from Western Union could be pedaling up to their house right this very minute.

One by one, the mourners followed Reverend Schuyler, filing by to say a few words to the McKelveys, still seated in the front pew. Ellie listened, in spite of herself. The boy with the grandmother turned out to be the newsboy at Jimmy's trolley stop downtown.

"Mr. Jim always said 'Keep the change, kiddo.' " The boy's lower lip trembled. "I figured he'd lick them lousy Nazis." His grandmother hustled him along, mumbling condolences as she went.

Ellie twisted around to see how many people were waiting in line. A lot. We're never getting out of here, she thought. She snapped around to catch Sal pinching the inside of her arm.

"Ow! What'd you do that for?"

"Pay attention. People are trying to be nice."

Ellie sighed. She was hot and thirsty.

"Oh, run along," said Gramma. "Stretch your legs. Most of these folks will be coming by the house anyhow."

Relieved, Ellie concentrated on not running down the aisle. She knew there was a water fountain in the side vestibule.

By the fountain stood the colored girl, teetering on patent leather pumps.

"Hi," said Ellie as she dove for the spigot. After a couple of gulps, she raised her head. The girl was still there.

"You must be Mr. Jim's sister," she said. "Y'all look alike. Same eyes."

"Yep. I'm Ellie. And you are . . . ?"

"Rose. I'm the elevator girl at Kaufmann's."

Ellie had never talked to a colored person and wasn't sure what to say. She settled on "That's nice."

"It's a fine job," the girl agreed. "Beats picking cotton back home."

"Where's home?"

"Alabama," said Rose. "My brother was working in the steel mill up here, and he sent for me. Said that there was all kinds of jobs for a smart colored girl."

"Your brother in the service now?" Ellie asked.

Rose nodded. "Yep. The Army. Joined the morning after Pearl Harbor."

"Is he in England?" said Ellie. "Maybe he saw Jimmy."

The girl shook her head. "He's at Fort Huachuca, Arizona."

"Arizona? We aren't fighting anybody in Arizona."

The girl studied her shiny shoes. "That's where the Army stuck most of the colored fellas. The ones that ain't cooks and porters and stuff. Leroy is smart and strong, but they got him marching around the desert. Army thinks coloreds are lazy and cowards."

"That's silly," said Ellie. "Anybody who works in a steel mill isn't lazy or a coward. How come he didn't go with the Marines? They're the tough guys," she added, thinking of the Gandeck brothers.

"Marines won't take no colored boys." Rose shrugged. "Leastways, he can't get in no danger out there." Her hands flew to her mouth. "Beg pardon. Didn't mean any disrespect to you or Mr. Jim."

"That's okay."

"Mr. Jim was a fine gentleman. Treated everybody the same. Most folks act like I'm part of the elevator, the buttons or the gate. But Mr. Jim always said 'Morning, Rose. Have a good day.' And in the evening, he'd say 'Time to head for the barn, Rose.'

"And them silly songs he used to sing." Rose smiled, although a tear trickled down the side of her nose. "That one about the lil fishies and the mama fishy too. And 'The Hut-Sut Song.' He was a happy man, your brother."

Ellie watched Rose dab her cheek with a flowered hanky, then give her nose a mighty honk. For a minute, she considered letting her in on her secret, that it had all been a terrible mistake.

Instead, she touched Rose's wrist just above her glove and said, "Thanks for telling me."

"You're welcome," said Rose. Ellie watched as she clicked down the hallway on her shiny heels. She turned at the door and gave a tiny wave.

The last mourner, Mrs. Corsiglia, was hugging Mama's neck and saying something in Italian as Ellie came back to the pew.

"Let's get a move on," said Toots. "Folks'll be waiting at the house."

Once out of the church, Ellie was surprised to see that the rest of the neighborhood was going about their usual Saturday morning business. Mothers with two-wheeled shopping carts going into the five-and-dime. Kids lining up for the Saturday matinee. She watched as the Hales and Corsiglias unlocked their stores and flipped the CLOSED signs to OPEN. The shopping-cart ladies moved quickly into the open stores. The DRINK COCA-COLA chalkboard at Green's announced that the New York Giants had beaten the Pirates yesterday, 0–4.

The McKelveys walked slowly down Macken Street, midday sun beating on their heads. Mom and Pop wore dazed, bewildered expressions as they walked arm in arm. Toots marched briskly ahead. Sal lagged behind with her girlfriends, who, for once, weren't giggling their heads off. Ellie brought up the rear with Gramma and Grampa.

Nobody had told her how hot nylons were, and she couldn't wait to get home and take them off. But Ellie forced herself to keep pace with her grandparents.

As Toots had predicted, people waited for them on the porch. But not Fred. Or Mr. Wheeler, or anyone else from Western Union.

The crowd in front of the living room window parted. The window with the service flag. The flag was still there. But the blue star was gone. Replaced with a gold one.

The bad-luck gold star of the dead.

No!

25

After a day or two, the neighbors carried home their cake plates and casserole dishes. Ellie took the funeral wreath off the front door. Sympathy cards trickled to a few, then one or two, then finally none. They piled up on the dining room table, unopened, gathering dust. The family ate in the kitchen.

The McKelveys went in and out by the back door. No one wanted to see the Christmas tree. Or Jimmy's portrait, back on the mantel. Or the mound of mail on the dining room table. When Ellie went out for the mail, she averted her eyes from the flag in the window.

Jimmy wasn't coming home. Ellie knew that, but her heart wouldn't listen. Back and forth, her heart and head argued.

First came hope. *If Fred would just come with that telegram . . .*

But when Fred didn't come, hope turned to frustration, then sadness.

She cried, but only in the bathroom with the shower on. But crying didn't give her that clean, relieved feeling. Just empty. Blank. Numb.

Slowly, the empty place filled with anger.

You lied, Jimmy. You let me think you'd be safe.

The anger kindled into a bonfire of rage. Ellie wanted to do horrible, terrible things. Stomp flowers. Smash windows. Slash furniture. Scream and scream until her throat bled.

Instead, she walked around feeling mean and hateful, wondering why some people lived and some people died.

"Hello, Ellie," Mrs. Schmidt called from her garden, her sunburned face glowing above the zinnias.

"Hi, Mrs. Schmidt." Ellie thought, *You're old. Why aren't you dead, instead of Jimmy?*

Buddy Gandeck huddled on his porch swing, wrapped in a wool blanket, even though it was a hot day. Ellie waved. He stared at her. No, not *at* her—*through* her, as if she were a ghost. You're alive and you don't even care, Mr. Big Hero. Victoria has four brothers. I have one. Why did mine have to die?

Ellie seethed, furious at everybody and everything.

Then, as suddenly as it came, the anger disappeared, leaving her exhausted and spent, and soon Ellie was crying in the bathroom again.

The rest of the McKelveys went about their business. Ellie would look around the supper table, at Mom passing the peas or Sal yattering about Connie Cavendish, and would want to shout, *What's wrong with you? Don't you know everything has changed?*

But no one talked about Jimmy. Or the war. Everyone spent as little time together as possible. Mom stayed up all night doing laundry, radio dance music pouring from the basement. Toots spent more and more time with the Bettys.

Pop never came home for supper, choosing to work later and later at the post office. When he did come home, he'd change clothes and go down to the park across from the school. Ellie and Stan followed him one night to see what he did there.

"Jeez, he's not doing anything," Stan whispered as they crouched in the picnic shelter, struggling to see in the dark. "Just wandering around."

Ellie supposed the park was better than Pop belting beers at the Do-Drop, but it was unsettling. She couldn't fall asleep until she heard him tiptoe up the creaky steps to his and Mom's room. It seemed no time at all before she heard him leave for work.

In a way, Ellie understood. Being together reminded them of Jimmy. Talking about Jimmy hurt too much. *Thinking* about Jimmy hurt too much. She would hear "The Hut-Sut Song" or see Lana Turner in a magazine and think *Jimmy!* Then a door would slam in her head.

Time to cry in the bathroom again.

————

Hard as she tried to ignore it, Ellie always caught a glimpse of gold star whenever she passed the service flag. One day, when she was home alone and could stand it no longer, she snatched it out of the window. She couldn't scream or swear or slam things, but she could get rid of that hateful flag.

Ellie tried to rip it in two, but the fabric was too strong. She could cut it into little pieces and burn it. But somehow she just couldn't do it. *Not just now. I'll do it later.*

She ran upstairs and stuffed it under her mattress.

One hot August morning, Ellie went to bring in Pop's *Post-Gazette*—and stepped into a sea of jars. The stairs, porch, and the terrace walk were covered with canning jars. Dozens and dozens of jars. Tomatoes and pickles and beans. Jars of things Mom never canned . . . plum preserves and apple jelly and piccalilli.

"We have such good neighbors," said Mom as she and Sal helped Ellie carry the jars to the storage cellar. "We have much to be thankful for."

Ellie looked at Mom, her hair sticking every which way, a splotch of something brown on her wrinkled housedress. Ellie knew Mom said these words because they were the right ones to say.

Not because she thought they were true.

Three weeks after Ellie's birthday, Mom went back to work.

"I need to go," she said, retrieving her lunch bucket from the kitchen cabinet. "Maybe my little effort will help some other mother's son. I wish I could make a dent in the

. . . the letters in the dining room." Mom's voice faltered. "So many nice people, and I just can't . . ."

"Don't worry," said Toots. "Me and the girls can take care of them."

Which was why Ellie was sitting at the dining room table one sticky afternoon with Sal and Toots, a fountain pen, a bottle of ink, and a stack of thank-you cards. The room had been shut up since the funeral, and smelled faintly of fried chicken and pierogies.

"Aren't you supposed to be at work?" Ellie asked Sal.

"Mr. Green says I should take off whenever I need to." Sal blew at a stray lock of hair. "Here." She shoved a stack of envelopes at Ellie.

Ellie's cards all had crosses and lilies and flowery verses about "your time of sorrow" and were from people she didn't know. Pop's post office pals, Mom's fellow plant workers, parents of Sal's friends. None of it had anything to do with Jimmy. Not the crosses or lilies or the people who'd never met him.

In her best penmanship, Ellie wrote *The McKelvey family thanks you for your kindness and prayers in our time of sorrow* on each note card. That's what Mom had written for them to copy. She carefully blotted the card and began another. *The McKelvey family thanks you* . . .

"Hey, this one is from England," said Sal. "Look at the stamps. I'll bet it's from those people Jimmy used to visit. What was their name?"

"Whitehurst," said Ellie.

Sal shook out a letter and read:

Dear Mr. and Mrs. McKelvey, Sal, Ellie, and Aunt Toots,

Please forgive my familiarity, but I feel as if I know you all. I was devastated to learn of Jimmy's death. He was a dear boy, so like my own Clive. I know he was a good son, a good brother, and a good friend, because he was all of those things to us. He always said, "You Brits are like Pittsburghers. You like bars and beer and a good time." It was always a good time when Jimmy was around. How we will miss him.

Sincerely,
Margaret Whitehurst

Ellie imagined Jimmy singing along to Cilla's accordion. "Mairzy doats and dozy doats and . . ."

Don't. Think. Hurts too much.

"Listen to this one," said Toots, waving a sheet of tablet paper.

Dear Mr. and Mrs. McKelvey,

I was in Jim's high school class and I wanted you to know what a good egg he was. I had polio as a kid. I get around OK on crutches, but I never could do the things the other fellows could. Sometimes they gave me a hard time. Jim looked out for me, not making a big fuss, but just including me. Everyone liked him, so if Jim McKelvey thought I was OK, everyone else thought so too. I heard Jim was a medic. That's him all over, always thinking of the other fellow. For the rest of my life, whenever I see someone in trouble I'll ask myself "What would Jim do?"

Sincerely,
Howard (Howie) Ellsworth

"That's Jimmy all right," sighed Toots. "Always looking out for the little guy."

Ellie ripped into an envelope and pulled out linen stationery printed, *Women's Auxiliary Volunteer Emergency Service, WAVES Barracks, Washington, D.C.*

"Who's that from?" Sal asked.

"Miss Ruthie." Ellie read slowly, trying to make out the ornate script.

Dear McKelveys,

I am so sad for you. Jimmy was good to Papa and me. He did so many kindnesses, like shoveling coal into the cellar each winter, helping Papa fix this and that at the store. He never wanted thanks. "Neighbors help each other," he always said. Jimmy made you feel like you were the most important person in the world, and he meant it. He was no phony, Jimmy McKelvey. God rest his soul.

Ruth Greene, Specialist, First Class, WAVES

"Wow," said Sal softly. "I didn't know he did all that. He never said anything."

"That's the kind of fella he was," said Toots, wiping her eyes. "Never made a fuss, never wanted one made over him."

Ellie's pen moved across card after card, but her mind was far away. *All these people loved Jimmy, too, in ways and for things we never knew.*

As the afternoon ticked on, reading and sharing the letters, it was as if Jimmy still lived. Ellie half expected him to bang through the screen door, yelling, "I'm starving. What's for supper?"

But of course, she now knew that wasn't going to happen.

The McKelvey family thanks you . . .

26

Ellie's days muddled together in a gray, steamy string. August day followed August day, marching relentlessly toward Labor Day, and the start of school.

To the rest of the world, Ellie looked like the same old Ellie. She heard people whispering about her at church, at the grocery store, at the movies.

"That Ellie McKelvey is a tough cookie," they said. "Never shed a tear. What a trouper."

If they only knew, thought Ellie. But they were right. No one would ever see her shed a tear.

Ellie was sorting laundry in the cellar when Toots clumped down the stairs in her work boots.

"Hey, Short Stuff, here's my two cents' worth for the wash." Toots slung a laundry bag in Ellie's direction.

"Gee, thanks," Ellie muttered as she dumped it out. "Just what I need."

But Toots didn't hear her. "There's a rumor that North-side Market has meat," she shouted over the *chuggeda-chuggeda* of the washing machine. "I'm going to see what's there. I'll be back to make supper."

"Okay." Ellie didn't look up from the pile of dirty clothes as Toots left. One red sock in a load of whites, and the McKelveys would all be sporting pink underwear.

White shirt, this pile. Overalls, that pile. Red socks, bandanna, Jimmy's Hawaiian shirt.

Jimmy's shirt? What was it doing in the wash? She squinted at the wrinkled cloth. What was that? She held the shirt to the ceiling light bulb.

There, on the left sleeve, a big blotch covered an entire hula girl. Ellie sniffed the spot, then rubbed it. Machine oil. Toots must have worn it to work.

Oil on Jimmy's special shirt. Oil that wouldn't come out. Not even if Ellie used a scrubbing board, a whole box of Rinso, and all her strength.

Ellie's smoldering anger turned to rage. Toots would be gone for at least an hour. Plenty of time for what Ellie had in mind.

Calmly, she piled the freshly ironed sheets and table-cloths into the laundry basket and carried it upstairs to the kitchen linen cupboard. She neatly stacked the sheets on the shelves, tablecloths in the drawers. The quiet *click* of the cupboard doors closing set the bonfire in Ellie's heart roaring.

She pounded upstairs and threw open Toots's door with

a bang. For a second, she was surprised the room didn't fight back or burst into flames. But no, it was the same old messy, smoky-factory-smelling room that said Toots lives here now.

You ruined Jimmy's shirt. Not your shirt. Jimmy's. Not your room. Jimmy's.

Ellie set about removing all traces of Toots. She jerked open the top dresser drawer. *Crash! Dump.* Toots's bobby socks and brassieres scattered across the floor. But what was this on top?

An opened letter from Jimmy's friend Max. Ellie shook it from the envelope. She meant to scatter the pages, and douse them with Evening in Paris, but Jimmy's name caught her eye.

August 1, 1944

Dear Agnes,

I know you folks have heard about Jimmy's death by now. If anyone feels worse about this than you, it would have to be me. Jim was a good person, and a true friend. He might still be alive right now if he hadn't been so unselfish.

Jim wanted to save everybody. One by one, those damned Germans picked off us medics, aiming for the red cross on our helmets. Before long, it was just me and Jim, and about a million Germans, it seemed, shooting at us. If only we'd had guns. I got hit in the shoulder. Jim started to cart me off to an aid station when one caught him square in the helmet. He died fast. The last thing he said was "You're going to be OK, Max." And he was gone.

There's talk of putting Jim up for a medal, besides the Purple Heart. The Medal of Honor wouldn't be enough to show how brave and good he was.

I'm already back in the battle, though I can't tell you where. I just know that I have to keep fighting for Jim. For you. For all the fellows who can't anymore.

Max

"And he was gone." Gone?

Ellie crumpled the paper. Her thoughts disappeared in a frenzy of motion. Black buzzing spots sizzled before her eyes, like angry bees. Far away, Ellie heard things crashing and breaking, blood pounding in her ears. After what seemed a long time, she knew she was tired. Very, very tired. The angry bee-things went away, and she could see again.

Someone had tossed Toots's belongings around the room. Spilled bottles. Thrown powder. Strewn her clothes hither and yon. Dresser drawers on the floor, bedclothes ripped from the mattress, lamp tipped over.

Ellie guessed that someone was she. But she didn't really care.

Her hands were full. What was this?

One clutched Jimmy's leather jacket. The other, something wrapped in tissue. Some forgotten Christmas present? She unwrapped the tissue. Her ashtray. Where did that come from? Why is it wrapped so carefully? Where did I find the jacket?

Throwing herself across her own bed, Ellie fell asleep, inhaling the leather-and-Vitalis scent of Jimmy's jacket.

A shadow fell across Ellie's bed. Toots. *Uh-oh* . . .

But Toots didn't look particularly angry.

"If you're over your hissy fit, you can put my things back where you found them," she said. "When you're done, come on down to the kitchen. Got something for you."

Slowly, Ellie set Toots's things to rights. She couldn't imagine what Toots might have for her, unless it was a punch in the kisser. She worked steadily, refolding clothes in the drawers, wiping up spilled perfume and powder.

Finally, Ellie finished. Not knowing what to expect, she went down to the kitchen.

Toots stood at the counter, a butcher knife flashing through a skinny-looking chicken.

"Chicken," she said without turning around. "Northside had chicken."

Ellie hesitated at the door. She didn't want to get too close to that knife.

"There's a letter for you on the table. Don't know how you missed it. Lord knows you found everything else in my room." Toots gestured over her shoulder with the knife. "Didn't give it to you earlier, because I didn't think you were ready for it."

"What do you mean, not ready for it?" Ellie asked.

Toots turned to face her. "If I'da given you the letter at the first, you wouldn'ta taken in what it said. You was too mad."

"Really? How could you tell?"

"The look in your eye, for one thing. The way you clenched your jaw, for another. Like you was holding something in. Judging by the wreck you made of my room"—Toots chuckled a little—"I reckon you got all the mad out of you. You read the letter now. Might answer a few questions for you."

An envelope leaned against the salt and pepper shakers. *For Ellie*, it said. In Jimmy's handwriting.

Ellie's heart shot up to her throat, thumping wildly. With shaking hands, she unfolded the letter.

Dear Movie Star,

If you're reading this, then you know what happened. I wanted to set a few things straight with you.

I know I promised that nothing would happen to me. I shouldn't have done that. Some promises are not ours to make. Sometimes you go ahead and make them anyway and hope for the best. You don't want the people you love to worry. I'm sorry, Movie Star.

I wanted to be there for all the important stuff in your life. The first day of high school and your first date. Graduation and getting married. But I'm not sorry that I came over here. I don't want some crazy guy like Hitler taking over the world. There are worse things than dying. Like knowing you could've done the right thing . . . and you didn't. Like not really living while you are alive. I'm just sorry I'm not coming home.

I won't be around in the flesh, but you know I'll always be there. Just look in your heart, and I will always be there. And if you listen real hard, you will hear me saying, "I'm proud of you, Movie Star. You're doing fine."

Be a good girl, and help Mom and Pop all you can.

Love always, Jimmy

P.S. Don't forget to let the joy out.

P.P.S. In case you're wondering, I gave your birthday card to Mrs. Whitehurst to send for me. I sent this letter to Toots a while back, just in case.

Ellie folded the letter back into the envelope and waited for something to happen. Tears? No, she was all cried out. Anger? No, she had taken all that out on Toots's belongings. Slowly, Ellie climbed the stairs to her room. Reaching under her mattress, she drew out the service flag. She smoothed out the wrinkles as she hung it back in the living room window. Then she went out on the porch to see if she had hung it straight.

She had.

"Sal's been telling everybody at Green's that Jimmy's gonna get a medal," Jellyneck said to Ellie a few days later. "That's good." He sounded wistful. "Does it make a difference?"

"Does what make a difference?" Ellie asked.

Jellyneck gulped. "Well, you know. That your brother died a hero instead of uh . . ."

"In a jeep accident," Ellie finished in a flat voice. "No. It doesn't make one bit of difference. He's still dead."

"I thought so. Just wondered."

27

Labor Day dawned broiling hot.

"When are we leaving for West View Park?" Ellie asked for the fifth time.

"I'm tempted to spend the day sleeping," said Mom, yawning as she packed the picnic basket.

"Not really?" said Sal and Ellie together, horrified.

"Of course not. What kind of person spends the day in bed? Still . . . a few extra hours of sleep . . ."

"Sleep on a holiday?" Toots bounded downstairs, wide awake for once, in a new cherry print dress. It always gave Ellie a start to see Toots in anything other than her work clothes. Overalls suited her better, somehow.

"Sit down and eat breakfast, all of you. Nobody's going anywhere until after breakfast." Mom plopped the Shredded Wheat box on the table.

Twirl-twirl. The doorbell.

"I'll get it." Ellie jumped up from the table. Eating Shredded Wheat seemed like too much work today.

Stan and Jellyneck stood on the porch, spit-and-polished.

"What are you two doing here?" asked Ellie.

"Ma stayed up so late canning, she and Dad aren't going until lunchtime," said Stan. "She said I could go with yunz if it's okay with your folks."

"And me, too," added Jellyneck, in case Ellie was wondering.

A half hour later, Ellie sat squished between the boys on the Number 10, watching Mom and Pop, who sat across from her. Mom had combed her hair, put on a fresh dress and lipstick. But her hair looked dull, the dress limp, the lipstick too bright on her pale face. Pop's face was gray, and his shoulders hunched. Another night wandering around the park, Ellie figured. But when we get to West View, things will be just like they used to be.

"Where's Sal?" Stan asked. "Isn't she coming?" He sounded disappointed.

Ellie gave a short laugh. "Are you kidding? She wouldn't be caught dead with us. She is coming later with Connie Cavendish and the rest of her birdbrained friends."

Mom craned her head around the car, then leaned toward Ellie, face puzzled.

"Where's Toots?" she asked. "I don't see her."

"Don't you remember?" Ellie said, trying not to yell in the crowded car. "She left early to meet up with Wally and the Bettys."

Mom's blank expression told Ellie that she did not. Ellie sighed.

"We're all getting together for lunch, down by the bandstand."

"Oh, okay." Mom smiled, her puzzled expression relaxing.

Labor Day was another free-tickets-for-kids day at West View, only this time it was the labor unions handing them out. Again, the three friends took turns collecting extra tickets.

But the fun had gone out of it for Ellie. Each time she rode a ride or won a Kewpie doll she thought, The last time I did this, Jimmy was still alive. Finally, Ellie gave the rest of her tickets to the boys, telling them that she was going to sit with her parents and Toots.

"Yunz kidding?" Jellyneck said. "You'd rather listen to them clowns give speeches than ride the Dips?" Not that he waited for an answer. He and Stan were off with their fistfuls of tickets before Ellie could say boo.

She was sorry as soon as they had left. She found her parents and Toots and curled up on the wash-worn quilt, watching ants invade the picnic basket. It was election year, and it seemed like everyone from the mayor to the dogcatcher made a speech that day.

Ellie was half-asleep when she heard "Let not these brave men have died in vain." She sat up. The speaker, a red-faced man, was thundering into a screeching microphone and waving his hammy hands. "Let not their memory vanish in the mists of history."

The words shot through Ellie's head like lightning. For the first time in weeks, her brain felt clear, and she could think. Her heart thudded, the soft quilt beneath her legs seemed to give way, as if she were shooting down the steepest drop on the Dips. Overhead, the sky swirled hot and blue.

Like the steady tapping of a telegraph, the thought marched letter by letter through Ellie's head. *I'm forgetting Jimmy because I'm afraid to remember. It's too painful.*

There are worse things than dying, Jimmy had said. *Like not really living while you are alive.*

She closed her eyes and felt the hot breeze on her face. The screams from the Dips, the carousel music, the shouting politician faded away. High above it all, she heard the faint *ding-ding* of the Number 10, unloading more picnickers, taking home the early leavers.

Flash! And there was Jimmy, lightly leaping from the top step of the Number 10, jacket over one arm, the *Sun-Telegraph* tucked under the other. "Hi, Movie Star," he called.

Tears prickled Ellie's closed lids. *This hurts so much. I can't do this. But if I don't, it will be as if Jimmy never lived at all.*

She took a shaky breath and let the memory come. It had been a summer's evening at the trolley stop. Just an ordinary evening. Jimmy's eyes shining like her best blue marbles. The smell of street asphalt, and creosote beading on the telephone poles. Mr. Green sweeping his walk. "You two looking for a cold pop before supper?"

238

"Maybe later," Jimmy answered, jingling the coins in his pocket. He squeezed Ellie's arm, and she knew that at that moment, she was the most important person in Jimmy's world.

She opened her eyes. The earth felt firm beneath her legs again, the sky steady. And the sore spot on her heart not quite so sore.

Ellie rolled over to look at Mom, listening to the politician, but with that same vague otherworldly look in her eyes. Rising up on her elbows, she started to tell Mom what had happened, but stopped. *She'll have to figure it out for herself. Pop, too.* There was something else Ellie needed to do, and now. But not alone.

Toots sprawled on the blanket, arms under her head, hat covering her face. Lifting the brim, Ellie whispered in her ear. Her aunt sat up, smiling. "You got it, kiddo. Let me get my things together, and we'll go."

As Toots gathered her belongings, Ellie took one last look at all the things she loved: the Dips, the game stands, the merry-go-round cranking out "My Wild Irish Rose." She knew it would never be the same to her again. West View was a place where children had no cares.

And she wasn't a child anymore.

28

hat does it," said Toots as Ellie closed the last box.

They stood in the living room, gazing at the now-naked Christmas tree. Home from the picnic, they had set to work, gingerly lifting the glass balls from the brittle branches. Unwinding the garlands. Taking down Jimmy's tin star from the top.

"Not much left, is there?" said Ellie. Without the decorations, the tree was little more than a pole and twigs, the last needles vacuumed up months ago.

"Nope," said Toots. "Nature didn't mean for it to sit in a house for months on end. Don't just stand there gawking." She swiped her damp forehead with her wrist. "Let's haul this thing out to the ash pit."

"We're going to burn it?" Ellie's throat tightened.

Toots hoisted the tree to her shoulder. "You got any better ideas?"

"It seems kind of . . . well . . . you know?" It was one thing to take the tree down, but burn it?

"Ellie." Toots's usually rough voice sounded soft. "It's just a tree. Or was. Let's put the poor thing out of its misery."

So that's what they did.

Sprawled on the back stoop, Ellie watched the last sparks from the burn barrel flitter over the alley. The restless feeling she had at the park returned.

The peaceful sounds of late afternoon washed over her. The shrill of cicadas. The faint mumble of a radio. Bikes racing up the street, baseball cards clicking on the spokes. With a steady stream of backfire, an old clunker of a car slowly turned the corner.

A breeze blew light and cool against Ellie's bare legs. Soon it would be time to put away her shorts. Tomorrow she would be a seventh grader. Had it been only a year since Jimmy had gone away? It seemed like a million years. It seemed like yesterday.

Ellie waited for the familiar pain. *He's in my heart,* she reminded herself. Every day it would hurt less, and she would remember more.

Gradually she became aware of shouting across the alley, at the Gandecks'. Why weren't they at the picnic? Ellie wondered. Everybody went to the Labor Day picnic.

Crash! Thud! Big noises, like thrown furniture. Screams. Not Mrs. Gandeck or Victoria.

A man. A man screaming.

The Gandecks' back door banged open, and Victoria came flying out.

Right behind her, Buddy, brandishing a knife. A big, curved knife.

Hot on their heels, Mr. and Mrs. Gandeck, huffing and puffing, never getting close to their son.

Ellie remembered Buddy's letter. *I got enough native knives and daggers to arm the whole sixth grade.*

"Run, Victoria!" Mrs. Gandeck shrieked.

Victoria ran, her long legs keeping her just ahead of Buddy. Once around the garage, twice. The third time, she made a break for the alley, but Buddy trapped her by the rubbish barrel. He screamed a long string of gibberish that Ellie couldn't make out, except for "Jap." He slashed the air with the knife.

"Oh no," Ellie breathed. "Run, Victoria."

But Victoria couldn't. She crouched in a wrestler's stance as Buddy feinted this way and that. Back and forth. Side to side, in a shadow dance. They froze, panting, eyes locked.

"Aiee!" Buddy wailed, as if tormented by a thousand demons. He heaved the rusty trash barrel. Victoria dodged, vaulted the fence, and dashed across the alley. Ellie ran to open the gate.

"Here," she said, drawing Victoria into the yard.

The McKelveys' back door banged open. Toots stepped out, dishcloth in hand.

"What the hell is going on?" she asked.

"Buddy," gasped Ellie, waving wildly toward the Gandecks' yard, where Buddy now had his parents backed against the garage.

Charging through the open gate, Toots sailed over the Gandecks' fence and took a flying leap onto Buddy's back, dishcloth still in hand. He wilted in a heap. Toots snatched the knife from the ground while Mr. and Mrs. Gandeck pounced on him, dragging his limp body toward the house.

Ellie led Victoria to the house, as if she were a lost toddler. "Sit," she said, gently pushing her to the stoop. Victoria's shoulders heaved, face buried in her hands.

Big bad Victoria Gandeck, crying!

At last Victoria's sobs came to a hiccupy end.

"Well, go ahead," she said, swiping the tears with her palms. "Tell the whole school. I have it coming to me, after all the hooey I spread around. My brother the big hero." Then her defiance vanished, as she sat hunched, hugging her knees.

"Tell them what?" asked Ellie.

"Buddy," Victoria said in a flat voice. "He's different. He's not Buddy anymore."

"But at least he came home," said Ellie. "I'd give anything to have Jimmy back."

"That's what *you* say." Victoria sounded like her old self. "What if he was crazy?"

"Crazy?" Buddy didn't look exactly sane, but crazy?

"Yeah." Victoria rested her chin on a knee. "Battle fatigue, they call it. Or shell shock. Whatever they call it, it makes people loony. See and hear things that ain't there. Like Japs and booby traps and people without heads and such."

"Oh." Ellie didn't know what to say.

"Like today. The docs told us not to startle him. No loud noises or nothing. But a car backfired while he was sleeping and he woke up screaming about Japs. Then he saw me, and thought *I* was a Jap. Dad was supposed to hide all those daggers, but I guess he missed one.

"Is he like that all the time?" Ellie couldn't imagine.

"Not all the time." Victoria sighed. "Sometimes he just sits in the front room, wrapped in his Marine blanket, rocking back and forth. We can talk till we're blue and he won't even blink."

"I'm sorry," said Ellie, although she wasn't sure that was the right thing to say. But Victoria went on as if she didn't hear.

"When he does talk he doesn't make any sense. Jabbering to men he thinks are there, and of course they ain't. Talking to ghosts or something."

"He's going to get better, isn't he?" asked Ellie. "I mean, it's not like he got shot in the head or something."

Victoria stared across the alley at her house. From inside came loud moans and thumping.

"I don't know," she said in a dull voice. "Sometimes I wish he *had* been shot in the head. You take out the bullet and sew 'em up and they either get better or die. The docs don't know what to do for Buddy, besides give him calming-down medicine."

"Well, that's something," said Ellie.

Victoria gave a short, ugly laugh. "Yeah, it calms him down all right. He conks out for days. Or he stares into space and staggers around like he's drunk. We don't use the medicine except for emergencies. Like today."

"Why doesn't he just go back to the hospital?" Ellie asked.

"All they'll do is give him a bunch of drugs and let him wander around the loony ward. Do you know there are men like Buddy who have been there since the *last* war?"

Ellie counted quickly in her head. "But that's twenty-five years, give or take a little!"

"Uh-huh," said Victoria. "Ma says if Buddy's gonna be out of his head, he might as well be among people who love him. She thinks he's gonna get better."

"What do you think?" asked Ellie.

"I don't know," said Victoria in a tiny voice. "I *want* him to get better."

"But you still have your other brothers. Frankie and George and . . ."

"I know," said Victoria. "But I was special to Buddy. I mean I still am . . ." Victoria's voice trailed off.

Ellie touched her shoulder gently. "It's okay," she said. "I know what you mean."

Someone at the Gandecks' snapped on a radio. Kate

Smith singing "God Bless America" drowned out whatever else was going on over there.

"It doesn't seem fair." Victoria fiddled with her frayed shoelaces. "Our brothers do what they think is right, and this is what happens."

"Yeah," Ellie agreed.

Victoria pounded a fist on her knee. "It ain't fair. It ain't. Buddy's the strongest guy I know. Nothing hurt him. Nothing stopped him. Until the Japs." She pounded harder. "I thought my brother was stronger and smarter than anyone."

"Yeah." Ellie chewed her knuckle. "Jimmy promised he'd be okay. That he'd come home. I mean, if you can't count on your brother, who can you count on?"

The girls watched Dr. Atkinson's shiny Lincoln bump down the alley, stopping at Victoria's driveway. He hustled through the kitchen door, doctor's bag in hand.

"You know what? Everybody will go on with their lives and forget what Buddy and Jimmy and all the others did. Nobody thanked 'em or anything," Victoria said.

"I don't think they did it for the thanks," said Ellie. "They went because they wanted to. Because they thought it was the right thing to do. Commando Kelly got parades and speeches and a key to the city, and he said all he wanted was to go home."

"Buddy and Jimmy didn't even get to come home." Victoria sighed. "Well, Buddy's home, but he don't know it. Not really. And who's going to remember what they did?"

"We are," said Ellie.

"So?" Victoria shrugged. "What can we do?"

"Make a start." Ellie stood, and held out her hand to Victoria. "Come on in the house with me. I have to get something."

29

Nearer, My God, to Thee" pealed from the carillon as the girls crossed the schoolyard. Tree shadows stretched across the asphalt, still sticky from the heat.

"It's like walking on flypaper," Victoria complained, examining her tar-stained sneaker soles. She squinted up at the school windows. "Do you think anyone is here? School hasn't started yet."

"Yeah, but it does tomorrow," said Ellie. "Look, there's a light in Miss Deetch's office. I'll bet Miss Granberry's here, too."

"Well, that's teachers for you. Don't they know *nobody* works on Labor Day?"

The halls smelled of freshly waxed floors and last year's dust.

"Does the ceiling look lower to you?" Ellie whispered. Talking out loud didn't seem right, somehow.

"Yeah," Victoria agreed. "Do you think it shrunk over the summer? We didn't change *that* much, did we?"

Through the open office door, the girls spied Miss Deetch at her battleship desk, the lamplight sparkling on her dress lapel. Ellie caught her breath—the rhinestone eagle brooch.

"Hi, Miss Deetch," Victoria called.

The principal looked up, startled. Then she smiled. "Homesick already?"

Miss Deetch made a joke! Maybe principals were friendlier when you weren't their problem anymore.

"We have something for Miss Granberry," said Ellie, feeling braver.

"Well, she's in her room," said Miss Deetch. "You haven't forgotten the way already, have you?" Were her eyes twinkling? Or was it just the light reflecting from her spectacles?

"No, ma'am," said Ellie. Her eyes strayed to the principal's shoulder. "Miss Deetch, have you heard from your nephew? The one who gave you the eagle?" She held her breath.

Miss Deetch's face broke into such a wide grin, she looked almost . . . young.

"How dear of you to ask," she said. "We did hear from Ronnie. He is in a Japanese POW camp, but he writes that he is well. Time will tell."

"I'm glad, ma'am," said Ellie.

"Me, too," Victoria chimed in.

A shadow passed over the principal's face. "Eleanor, I was sorry to hear about James. It must be a comfort that he died a hero. I understand there is talk of a Bronze Star."

"Yes, ma'am." Someday, she would tell Miss Deetch that it wasn't the Bronze Star that comforted her.

"Victoria, how is your brother Edgar?"

Who's Edgar? Ellie wondered. Suddenly, she realized that Buddy Gandeck had lived across the alley her whole life and she'd never known his real name was Edgar.

Victoria paused. "He's doing about as good as the doctors expect."

"I hope he makes a full recovery," said Miss Deetch. She smiled at the girls. "We are so proud of our Macken Street boys. Let me show you something." She led the way to the entry hall and pointed to a tarnished plaque, the inscription barely visible. Ellie had passed it every day for seven years . . . and never once stopped to read it.

OUR HEROES WHO SERVED IN THE GREAT WAR. Underneath, a list of names. Stars next to the ones who had died.

Jelinek, Ignatz. Jellyneck's father? Uncle? *Corsiglia, Salvatore.* Mr. Corsiglia, the grocer. *McKelvey, Robert.* Pop? Ellie knew he had been in the Great War, but Pop never talked about it.

"The Veterans of Foreign Wars put up this tablet after the last war," said Miss Deetch. She smiled sadly. "It sounds strange to say 'the last war.' We thought the Great War was the war to end all wars."

But there *was* another war, Ellie thought. Could there be another war after this one? It would mean that Jimmy and all the other boys dying didn't count for anything.

Miss Deetch went on. "The Veterans will add another tablet when this war is over."

"That's nice," said Ellie, to be polite. But inside she shivered, imagining another tablet, with more names. And another and another . . .

"Well, have a nice visit with Miss Granberry," said Miss Deetch with a dismissive wave. "A principal's work is never done." She chuckled at her own joke as she disappeared into the office.

Ellie and Victoria climbed the stairs, sneakers squeaking on the waxed wood. The second-floor rooms were dark, doors closed. Mrs. Miller's service flag still had a blue star, Ellie was happy to see.

Suddenly, Victoria burst out. "What about *my* brother? Is Buddy's star going to be on that new tablet?"

"But he's not dead," Ellie pointed out.

"Oh yes he is," Victoria shot back. "He may be breathing and walking around, but the real Buddy died someplace in the Pacific and he isn't ever coming back."

Light spilled from Room Seven's open door, a bright patch in the dark hall. Inside, Miss Granberry, in her faded, flowered work smock, fussed with her African violets. Funny, just as the school seemed to have shrunk over the summer, Miss Granberry appeared bigger, stronger. Yet she still had to raise the watering can shoulder-high to reach the windowsill. How can that be? wondered Ellie. The whole world has changed . . . and it hasn't.

The girls stood at the room's threshold, uncertain of what to do, what to say. So Ellie said the first thing that came to mind.

"You didn't leave the violets here all summer, did you?"

Miss Granberry turned, a tiny smile making cat-whisker wrinkles around her mouth. "How nice to see you, Eleanor. No, I took my plants home over the summer." She looked over the top of her spectacles. "Nice to see you as well, Victoria."

"Hello, Miss Granberry," said Victoria. The last time she had spoken that quietly had been at Jimmy's wake.

Miss Granberry stowed the watering can in the supply cupboard. "And to what do I owe the honor of this visit?" She didn't sound sarcastic; she sounded like Miss Granberry.

"Do you still have the wall with all the pictures?" asked Ellie. She could see the picture-covered wall right in front of her, but Ellie didn't know how else to begin.

"Yes," said Miss Granberry. "I have added quite a few more over the summer, I am sorry to say."

The photographs now extended past the sides of the blackboard to the top, near the ceiling. How did the tiny teacher manage to tack them up there? Ellie took a deep breath and plunged ahead. "I have this picture of Jimmy and . . ."

"You would like to put it with the others," Miss Granberry finished for her. "Would you like to write something on the picture?" she added, offering her fountain pen.

In her best handwriting Ellie wrote *James McKelvey, died June 6, 1944, Omaha Beach, France. In the act of saving a friend.* She handed it to her teacher.

Miss Granberry blotted the ink, added a gold memorial star, then studied the wall before tacking it next to the Gandeck brothers.

"I think he'll feel at home next to the Gandecks, don't you?" said Miss Granberry.

Ellie nodded, not trusting herself to speak. Inside the picture, Jimmy smiled, one arm slung over Max's shoulder, one leg crooked, the other arm raised in a wave.

Look, Movie Star. I'm happy. You be happy, too.

Okay, Jimmy. Ellie winked at the picture. Did she imagine that Jimmy winked back?

Victoria spoke up. "Miss Granberry, could I add something to my brothers' picture?"

The teacher took down the color snapshot and handed it to her along with the pen.

"Could I have a gold star, too?" she asked. "I mean, *may* I have a star?"

The teacher neatly thumbed a gold star on the picture. Victoria's bold script sprawled across the margin. *Buddy Gandeck, lost, Tarawa Island, South Pacific, November 1943.*

Lost, thought Ellie. That's a good way to put it. Sometimes lost people find their way home.

"There," said Victoria with satisfaction. "Now they can't forget."

Miss Granberry smiled sadly. "Oh, my dear, but people *do* forget. It isn't the plaques and statues and medals that make people remember."

"It's not?" said Victoria. "What about the Sullivan brothers? And Commando Kelly? They'll be remembered forever."

Ellie thought about the plaque in the front hall . . . the one she had never read until today. "But they aren't braver than Buddy or Jimmy, are they? Just because those guys got a movie or a statue or a parade?" she said.

"Noooo," Victoria said, as if she were thinking hard. "But how will people remember without those things?"

"People will remember because *we* remember." Ellie grabbed Victoria's hands. "You and me. And Jellyneck. And Miss Granberry and her students. Because in our hearts they'll never die."

"Hunh?" Victoria's face was a question mark.

Ellie looked at Miss Granberry. "I don't know if I am saying it right."

Miss Granberry folded her hands against the faded roses of her smock. "You are saying it quite well, Eleanor. The stories you tell your children about your brothers will be worth more than parades or medals and folderol."

Through the open windows, the St. Matthew's bell chimed the half hour. Six-thirty. The rest of the McKelveys would be home from the picnic by now.

Miss Granberry heard it, too. "You girls need to scurry along to your suppers. We all need a good night's sleep for tomorrow."

Suddenly, Ellie didn't want to leave Room Seven and Miss Granberry.

And Jimmy.

"Your brothers are safe with me," Miss Granberry said, gently propelling them toward the door. "But you can come back and visit any time."

A calm came over Ellie. *Thank you, Jimmy. You did keep your promise. You are in my heart, for always.*

In the hall, the girls stopped short, enveloped in the golden glow of late afternoon coming through the stairwell windows.

"This is how I remember Buddy," Victoria said in a dreamy voice. "He taught me how to ice-skate and ride a bike and not to take nothing from nobody."

"So that's where you got that mean right hook," Ellie said, only half joking.

"You betcha!" Victoria socked her on the arm. "Buddy loved the Pirates and going to the Do-Drop with Pa after work. He was one tough Marine until he wore out."

A breeze rustled the treetops, cooling Ellie's warm neck.

"How about you?" Victoria asked.

Ellie watched the tree shadows ripple on the sidewalk.

Like swimming underwater, she thought. A million memories of Jimmy drifted by like schools of fish.

Leaning out the window, Ellie gulped the cooling air. "When I get married, I hope I have a boy, so I can name him Jimmy." She started for the stairs.

"But what are you going to *say* about Jimmy?" Victoria insisted.

Ellie paused on the top step, her hand on the sun-warmed stair railing. She grabbed for one of those happy memories now racing through her head like a sped-up movie.

"The banister," she said.

Victoria blinked in surprise. "The what? I was talking about Jimmy."

"So'm I," Ellie replied. She waved toward the wide oak balustrade curving away from them to the ground floor. "You ever think of taking the short way down, if you know what I mean?"

Victoria grinned. "Every day. You?"

"Yep. You ever do it?"

"Nope. How 'bout you?"

"No. But Jimmy did, once. He always said, 'You have to let the joy out.' "

Victoria and Ellie looked at each other, then at the polished banister, burnished bronze in the afternoon light.

Find the joy, Movie Star.

Ellie hopped on the banister and sailed down the shining expanse of oak. The knot of pain inside her eased. It would never go away, not altogether. But she knew the hurt would never be as strong again.

"Hey," she called up to Victoria. "Do you know the words to 'Mairzy Doats'?"

Acknowledgments

I could not have written this story without the collective memory of my personal platoon of "The Greatest Generation": Roy and Frances Rodman, John Downing, William Neofes, Sarah O'Brien, Georgia Scott, Eloyd Baldwin. Special thanks to my cousins Harriet Newton, Walter and Wilma Scott, and Melissa Neofes Mischak, who shared family stories, pictures, and letters. Thanks as well to my first readers, from Ms. Silber's fifth grade 2004–05, New Prospect Elementary, Alpharetta, Georgia: Joey Albano, Brian Dalluge, Michelle Demaline, Fred Hong, Ryan Quinn, and especially Josh Bugica.

Thank you, too, to my beloved Hive, especially Gretchen Will Mayo and Phyllis Harris, who read, advised, and kept me going. Last but not least, to the WINGS: Nancy Craddock, Connie Fleming, Maureen McDaniel, and Susan Rosson Spain, the best writers' group in Georgia.

12-08

OLD CHARLES TOWN LIBRARY
CHARLES TOWN, WV 25414
(304) 725-2208